OUTBACK KNIGHTS

Marriage is their mission!

From bad boys—to powerful, passionate protectors! Three tycoons from the Outback rescue their brides-to-be....

Meet Ric, Mitch and Johnny—once rebellious teenagers, they survived the Outback to become best friends and formidable tycoons. Now these sexy city hotshots must return to the Outback to face a new challenge: claiming their brides....

This month, it's sexy billionaire Johnny Ellis's turn

- *The Outback Marriage Ransom*
- *The Outback Wedding Takeover*
- *The Outback Bridal Rescue*

Emma Darcy is the award-winning Australian author of almost ninety novels for Harlequin Presents®.
Her intensely emotional stories have gripped readers around the globe.
She's sold nearly 60 million books worldwide and won enthusiastic praise.

"Emma Darcy delivers a spicy love story... a fiery conflict and a hot sensuality."
—*Romantic Times*

Dear Reader,

To me, there has always been something immensely intriguing about bad boys who've made good. With every possible disadvantage in their background, what was it that lifted them beyond it, that gave them the driving force to achieve, to soar to the heights of their chosen fields, becoming much more than survivors... shining stars?

In OUTBACK KNIGHTS, I've explored the lives of three city boys who ended up in juvenile court and were sent to an Outback sheep station to work through their sentences. There, at Gundamurra, isolated from the influences that had overwhelmed them in the past, and under the supervision and caring of a shrewd mentor, Patrick Maguire, the boys' lives became set on different paths as they learned how their individual strengths—their passions—could be used constructively instead of destructively.

But the big unanswered need is love. Even at the top it's lonely.

And it seemed to me beautifully fitting that as these boys had been rescued, so should they—as men—rescue the women who will give them love. I think there are times when all of us want to be rescued—to be cared for, protected, understood, made to feel safe. It's not that we can't manage independently, but, oh, for a knight in shining armor that will fight and slay our dragons with a passionate intensity that makes us melt!

Here they are—Ric Donato, Mitch Tyler and Johnny Ellis: OUTBACK KNIGHTS!

With love,

Emma Darcy

Emma Darcy

THE OUTBACK BRIDAL RESCUE

OUTBACK KNIGHTS

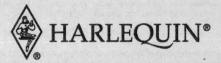

HARLEQUIN®

TORONTO • NEW YORK • LONDON
AMSTERDAM • PARIS • SYDNEY • HAMBURG
STOCKHOLM • ATHENS • TOKYO • MILAN • MADRID
PRAGUE • WARSAW • BUDAPEST • AUCKLAND

ISBN 0-373-12427-9

THE OUTBACK BRIDAL RESCUE

First North American Publication 2004.

www.eHarlequin.com

Printed in U.S.A.

PROLOGUE

Johnny Ellis
First Day at Gundamurra

THE plane was heading down to a red dirt airstrip. Apart from the cluster of buildings that marked the sheep station of Gundamurra, there was no other habitation in sight between here and the horizon—a huge empty landscape dotted with scrubby trees.

It made Johnny think of the old country ballads about meeting and overcoming incredible hardships in places such as this. And here he was, facing the reality of it for a while. Easy enough to see why the music for those ballads was always slow. Nothing fast going on down there.

'Wish I had my camera,' Ric Donato murmured.

The remark piqued Johnny's curiosity. Apparently the stark visual impact of the place didn't intimidate Ric, though like Johnny, he'd lived all his life in the city. It seemed odd that a thieving street-kid was into photography. On the other hand, the camera comment might simply be playing it cool, making a point of not letting any fear of what was waiting for them show.

Ric looked like he'd been bred from the Italian mafia, black curly hair, olive skin, dark eyes that flashed with what Johnny thought of as dangerous intensity, but if Ric Donato had come from that kind

5

of *family,* some smart lawyer would have got him off the charge of stealing a car and he wouldn't be on this plane with Johnny and Mitch.

'The middle of nowhere,' Mitch Tyler muttered dispiritedly, his eyes fixed on the same scene. 'I'm beginning to think I made the wrong choice.'

More gloom than cool from his other companion, Johnny thought, but then unlike himself and Ric, Mitch had a real family—mother and sister—and family couldn't visit him way out here. But choosing a year in a juvenile jail rather than the alternative sentence of six months working on a sheep station...

'Nah,' Johnny drawled with deep inner conviction. 'Anything's better than being locked up. At least we can breathe out here.'

'What? Dust?' Mitch mocked.

The plane landed, kicking up a cloud of it.

Johnny didn't care about a bit of dust. It was infinitely preferable to confinement. He hoped Mitch Tyler wasn't going to be a complete grouch for the next six months. Or a mean one, blowing up at any little aggravation. The guy had been convicted of assault. It might be true he'd only beat up on the man who'd date-raped his sister, but Johnny suspected that Mitch was wired towards fighting.

He had biting blue eyes, dark hair, a strong-boned face that somehow commanded respect. His build was lean though he had very muscular arms, and Johnny felt he might well be capable of powerful violence. Living in close quarters with him could be tricky if he didn't lighten up.

'Welcome to the great Australian Outback,' the cop escorting them said derisively. 'And just remember…if you three city smart arses want to survive, there's nowhere to run.'

All three of them ignored him. They were sixteen. Regardless of what life threw at them, they were going to survive. Besides, running would be stupid. Better to do the six months and feel free to get on with their lives, having served what the law court considered justice for their crimes.

Not that Johnny felt guilty of doing anything bad. He wasn't a drug dealer. He'd simply been doing a favour for the guys in the band, getting them a stash of marijuana to smoke after their gig at the club. They'd given him the money for it and the cops had caught him handing it over to the real dealer.

Impossible to explain he'd got the money from the musos. That would be dobbing them in and the word would go around the pop music tracks that he couldn't be trusted. Keeping mum and taking the fall was his best move. It was a big favour that could be called in when this stint on the sheep station was behind him, maybe get him a spot in a band playing guitar, even if he was only filling in for someone.

Johnny had learnt very young that pleasing people gave him the easiest track through life. It was much smarter to stay on their good side. Straying from that only brought punishment. He still had nightmares about being locked in a dark cupboard for upsetting his first foster parents. By the time he'd been placed in another home, he'd worked out how to act. It was a blueprint he always carried in his head—win friends, avoid trouble.

He hoped the owner of this place was a reasonable kind of guy, not some bastard exploiting the justice system to get a free labour force, just like some foster parents, taking money from the government for looking after kids who really had to look after themselves, in more ways than just earning their keep in those supposedly *safe* homes.

The judge had rambled on about this being a program that would get boys who'd run off the rails back to ground values, good basic stuff to teach them what real life was about.

As if they hadn't already had a gutful of real life! And its lessons!

Still, Johnny figured he could ride this through easily enough—put a smile on his face, roll his shoulders, act willing.

The plane taxied back to where a man—the owner?—was waiting beside a four-wheel-drive Land Rover. Big man—broad-shouldered, barrel-chested, craggy weathered face, iron-grey hair. Had to be over fifty but still looking tough and formidable.

Not someone to buck, Johnny thought, though size didn't strike fear in him anymore. He'd grown big himself. Bigger than most boys at sixteen. It made other guys think twice about picking a fight with him. Not that he ever actively invited one, and wouldn't here, either. A friendly face and manner always served him best.

'John Wayne rides again,' Mitch Tyler mocked, making light of the big man waiting for them, yet his body language yelled tension.

'No horse,' Johnny tossed at him with a grin, wanting Mitch to relax, make it easier for all of them.

It won a smile. A bit twisted but a smile nonetheless. It gave Johnny some hope that Mitch might loosen up, given time and if they were treated reasonably well here.

He caught Ric Donato looking curiously at him and wondered what he was thinking. Dismissing him as harmless? No threat? Possibly good company? What did he see?

Johnny tried envisaging himself objectively—a hunky guy who wouldn't be out of place in the front row of a football team, streaky brown hair that invariably flopped over his forehead because of a cowlick near his right temple, eyes that had a mix of green and brown in them and a twinkle of good humour that Johnny had assiduously cultivated, a mouth full of good white teeth which certainly helped to make a smile infectious.

Even so, he was no competition for Ric Donato in the good looks department. Girls probably fell all over him. Which was what had got him into trouble, stealing a Porsche to show off to some rich chick. Johnny had no time for girls yet. He just wanted to play his own music, get into a band, go on the road.

The plane came to a halt.

The cop told them to get their duffle bags from under the back seats. A few minutes later he was leading them out to a way of life which was far, far removed from anything the three of them had known before.

The initial introduction was ominous, striking bad chords in Johnny.

'Here are your boys, Maguire. Straight off the city streets for you to whip into shape.'

The big old man—and he sure was big close up—

gave the cop a steely look. 'That's not how we do things out here.' The words were softly spoken but they carried a confident authority that scorned any need for abusive tactics.

He nodded to the three of them, offering a measure of respect. 'I'm Patrick Maguire. Welcome to Gundamurra. In the Aboriginal language, that means "Good day." I hope you will all eventually feel it was a good day when you first set foot on my place.'

Johnny's bad feelings simmered down. It was okay. Patrick Maguire's little speech had a welcoming ring to it, no punishment intended. Nevertheless, a strong sense of caution had Johnny intently watching the big man's approach to Mitch, the first in line.

'And you are...?' The massive hand he held out looked suspiciously like a bone-cruncher.

'Mitch Tyler,' came the slightly belligerent reply. Mitch met the hand with his own in a kind of defiant challenge.

'Good to meet you, Mitch.'

A normal handshake, no attempt to dominate.

Johnny's smile was designed to disarm but it had more than a touch of relief in it as he quickly offered his hand in greeting, being next in line. 'Johnny Ellis. Good to meet you, Mr Maguire.'

The steely-grey gaze returned a weighing look that made Johnny feel he was being measured in terms far different to what he was used to. His stomach contracted nervously as the warm handclasp seemed to get right under his skin, seeking all he kept hidden.

His determinedly fixed smile evoked only a hint of amusement in the grey eyes, causing an unaccustomed sense of confusion in Johnny as Patrick

Maguire finally released his hand and moved on to Ric who introduced himself far more coolly, not giving anything away.

'Ready to go?' the old man asked him.

'Yeah. I'm ready.' Aggression in this reply.

Ready to take on the whole damned world if Ric had to, Johnny interpreted, and wondered if Patrick Maguire was looking for that kind of spirit. Had he himself failed some test by appearing too easygoing?

Didn't matter.

All he had to do was ride through the six months here with the least amount of trouble. He might not be a fighter like Ric and Mitch but he knew how to survive, and head-on clashes weren't his style. Reading the lay of the land, adjusting to it, accommodating it…that was the way to go for Johnny Ellis.

Yet as Patrick Maguire stood back and cast his gaze along the three of them, taking in his new recruits for outback tuition, he nodded, as though approving each one. Johnny's stomach relaxed, feeling good vibes coming from the man. Somehow he had passed the test, whatever it was. He was accepted.

So Gundamurra shouldn't be a bad place to be. The old man had said it meant "good day." Johnny decided he could do with a lot of good days. No worries. No stress. No angling for some step that would help him get where he wanted to go in the music world. He could let all that wait for six months, settle in and enjoy the wide open spaces.

Yeah…he was ready for this.

Probably more so than Ric or Mitch.

Though he hoped the three of them could establish and maintain friendly relations while they were here.

It was beyond Johnny Ellis's imagination that a friendship would evolve that would last the rest of their lives, intertwining through all that was important to them...being there for each other in times of need, understanding where they were coming from and why.

The bond of Gundamurra was about to be forged.

And at the heart of it was Patrick Maguire, the man who would become the father they'd never known, a man who listened to the people they were, learning their individual strengths, guiding them towards paths that could lead towards successful futures, encouraging them to fly as only they could... and always, always, welcoming them home.

CHAPTER ONE

Twenty-two years later...

JOHNNY ELLIS rode into the old western town that had been built for the movie. Behind him was the Arizona desert. In front of him was the film crew, cameras rolling. It was all he could do to keep a straight face, in keeping with the character he was playing—cowboy on a mission.

An inner grin was twitching at the corners of his mouth. On the country and western music scene, he'd made it to the top, selling umpteen platinum albums of his songs, but this was Johnny's first movie and he was having fun, doing something beyond even his wildest dreams.

Having learnt to ride at Gundamurra, he was a natural on a horse, and being big and tall—there weren't many movie stars with his physique—had snagged him the part. Of course, he did have a box-office name, too, a point his agent had made much of. Whatever...he was here doing it, and it sure tickled him to think of himself as following in John Wayne's footsteps.

Mitch and Ric had laughed about it, too.

But he had to be dead serious now. The cameras were zeroing in to do close-ups. Time to dismount, tie his reins to the rail, walk into the saloon, cowboy on a mission. This was the last take of the day, the light was right for it, and Johnny didn't want to mess it up. He was a professional performer, used to being onstage, and getting it right was second nature to him.

He didn't miss a step. The saloon doors swung shut behind him and the director yelled, 'Cut!' Johnny allowed himself a grin as he came back out to the street, confident there'd be no need to do this scene again. The grin grew wider when he spotted Ric Donato lurking behind the camera crew.

His old friend had made the time to come!

Johnny had invited him to the film set, the moment Ric had called to say he was in L.A., checking on that branch of his worldwide photographic business. It was a pity Lara and the kids weren't with him. Ric's wife was one lovely lady and their children had the trick of melting Johnny's heart, they were just so endearing. Little Patrick, who'd turned three just before last Christmas, would have loved a ride in the camera crane.

'Great to see you, Ric!' He greeted his old friend with immense pleasure. 'Want to be introduced around?'

'No.'

The quick and sober reply took Johnny aback. He instantly regrouped, seeing that Ric didn't look too good. In fact, he looked downright pained, something bad eating at him. No happy flash in his usually brilliant dark eyes. They were dull, sick.

'Could we go to your trailer, Johnny? Have some privacy?'

'Sure.'

He gestured the way and they walked side by side,

not touching. Any other time Johnny would have thrown an arm around Ric's shoulders, hugging his pleasure in his friend's company, but that didn't feel right, not with Ric so uptight and closed into himself. Johnny's stomach started churning. It always did when he sensed something bad coming.

He couldn't wait until they reached his trailer.

'What is it, Ric? Tell me!' he demanded grimly.

A deep, pent-up breath was expelled. 'I had a call from Mitch,' he stated flatly. 'Megan called him.'

'Megan Maguire?'

A vivid image of Patrick Maguire's youngest daughter instantly flew into Johnny's mind—a wild bunch of red curls, freckled face, eyes the grey of stormy clouds, always projecting fierce independence, spurning his every offer of help with work on the station, defying him to imply in any way that she wasn't fit and able to run Gundamurra just as well as her father did.

Which was probably true. She'd worked towards it, not wanting to do anything else with her life. Johnny knew he'd never made any criticism of that choice. He actually admired her very capable handling of the work she did. What he didn't understand was why she couldn't just ride along with his company whenever he visited, make him as welcome as her father did. She invariably shunned him as much as possible and when she couldn't, her scorn of *his* chosen career invariably slipped out.

Yet she'd liked listening to him play his guitar when she was a kid, hanging on his every word when he sang. Why she'd grown up into such a hard, judge-mental woman he didn't know, but be damned if he'd let her attitude towards him keep him away from Gundamurra. Patrick was like a father to him. Best father any guy could have.

'Patrick...' He felt it in his gut. 'Something's happened to Patrick.'

Another hissed breath from Ric, then... 'He's dead, Johnny.'

Shock slammed into his heart. His feet stopped walking. He shook his head, refusing to believe it. Denial gravelled from his throat as it started choking up. 'No...no...'

'Two nights ago,' Ric said in a tone that made the fact unequivocal, and he went on, quietly hammering home the intolerable truth. 'He died in his bed. His heart gave out. No-one knew until the next morning. Megan found him. Nothing could be done, Johnny. He was gone.'

Gone...

Leaving a huge black hole—a bottomless pit that Johnny kept tumbling down. He was barely aware of Ric's hand gripping his elbow, steering him. His feet moved automatically. He saw nothing. It wasn't until Ric thrust a glass of whisky into his hand that he realised he was sitting on the couch in the mobile home provided by the movie company.

'It's a hell of a blow. For all of us, Johnny.'

He nodded. Couldn't speak. Forced a swallow of whisky down his throat.

'I've booked flights to Australia for both of us. I guess you'll need to clear that with your people here. Might mean a delay in their schedule if they can't shoot around your absence.'

The movie...meaningless now.

The deep ache of loss consumed him. Ric had Lara and their children. Mitch had Kathryn, with a baby on the way. They'd both made homes of their own. For Johnny, Gundamurra and Patrick was home, and with Patrick gone…it was like having the roots of his life torn out of him.

There was no longer any reason for him to go back.

Megan wouldn't want him there.

But he had to go back this one last time…say goodbye to the man who'd always treated him as a son, even though he was no blood relation. Megan couldn't begrudge him that. Ric and Mitch would be there with him. All three of them, remembering what Patrick had given them…the big heart of the man…

Why had it stopped?

He looked up at Ric, his inner anguish bursting into speech. 'He was only in his seventies.'

'Seventy-four,' came the quiet confirmation.

'He was so strong. He should have lived to a hundred, at least.'

'I guess we all thought that, Johnny.'

'It's only been three months since Christmas. He looked well then. Same as ever.'

Ric shook his head. 'There were no warning signs. Maybe the stress of the drought, having to kill so many sheep, lay off staff…'

'I offered help. Whatever was needed to tide them over, see them through the drought however long it went on. You know I've got money to burn, Ric.'

Ric's mouth twisted into an ironic grimace. 'I made the same offer. Most likely Mitch did, too.'

'He helped us, dammit! Why couldn't he let us

help him?' Johnny's hands clenched. 'I bet it was Megan who wouldn't take what we offered. Too much damned pride. And Patrick wouldn't go against her.'

'Don't blame Megan, Johnny. She's got enough to carry without a load of guilt over her father's death. I'd deal kindly with her if I were you. Very kindly. Patrick would want you to.'

'Yes, I know, I know...' He unclenched his hands, opening them in a helpless gesture. 'I'll miss him.'

Ric nodded, looked away, but not before Johnny caught the sheen of moisture glittering in his dark eyes. It was a heart-twisting reminder that Patrick had been like a father to all three of them, not just him. Ric was hurting, too. And Mitch...

Mitch was probably already at Gundamurra, giving whatever support was needed, making the legal business of death as easy as he could. Being a top-line lawyer, he'd do that for Patrick's daughters. There wasn't just Megan to consider, but Jessie and Emily, as well. They'd all be in shock. Ric was right. Patrick would expect *his boys* to deal kindly with them.

'We don't know why he died,' Ric said brusquely. 'Maybe it was just...his time to go. No point in railing against it, Johnny. We've got to get moving to make the flights home. Are you okay to do whatever you've got to do before we leave?'

He gulped down some more whisky. It helped burn away the welling of tears behind his eyes. 'Ready to go,' he asserted just as brusquely, rising to his feet. 'Let me make a few calls first, clear the way.'

* * *

Helicopter to Phoenix, flight to Los Angeles…many hours passed before Ric and Johnny could finally board the Qantas jet to Sydney and settle in their seats for the longest leg of their journey over the Pacific Ocean. The flight steward offered them champagne. They both declined, choosing orange juice instead. It was not a time for champagne.

A question had been niggling at Johnny. 'Why didn't Mitch call me direct? It would have saved you coming to get me, Ric.'

'We thought it was better this way…the two of us travelling together.'

'Well, I'm glad to have your company but we could have linked up here for this flight.'

Ric slanted him a wry look. 'You might not have co-operated with that plan. You have a habit of doing things your own way. This course ensured I'd be with you.'

Johnny frowned. 'You thought I needed my hand held?'

'No. It's all a matter of timing. There's more, Johnny. Mitch didn't want to load it on you all at once over the phone. He gave that job to me with the advice to let you get over the shock of Patrick's death first.'

The nerves in his stomach started knotting up again. 'So hit me with *the more*. I'm sitting down and locked in. What else do I have to absorb?'

Ric looked at him, decided he was ready for it, and let him have it. 'Patrick's will. Mitch held it. He's opened it.'

'Well, that can't be bad.' Instant relief. 'Patrick was always fair.'

'Prepare yourself for another shock, Johnny. There's a huge mortgage on Gundamurra and you're about to inherit half of it.'

'What?' Incredulity blanked out several million brain cells.

'Not quite half. You get forty-nine percent of Gundamurra and Megan gets fifty-one, leaving her in the driver's seat where she's always expected to be. But she won't have expected to share her inheritance with you, Johnny. The normal thing would be a three-way split with her sisters.'

Co-owner of Gundamurra with Megan?

'Mitch thought you should be prepared…get your head around it before we arrive at Gundamurra,' Ric went on.

Johnny's head was spinning.

What did it mean?

Why would Patrick cut out his two older daughters?

Why make him co-owner rather than Ric or Mitch?

A sense of horror billowed through him. He reached out and gripped his friend's arm. 'I didn't ask for this, Ric. I swear I knew nothing about it.'

'I didn't think you did, Johnny,' Ric assured him. 'I have no doubt Patrick planned it himself.'

'But why me? It's not right, not…' His mind fumbled for words. 'Did he…did he explain to Mitch when he drafted the will?'

Ric shook his head. 'Mitch wasn't in on drafting

it. Patrick did it himself and sent it to him sealed for safe-keeping two months ago.'

'Two months…' Johnny shook his head in bewilderment. 'He must have made up his mind after Christmas.'

'Maybe he knew he didn't have long to live.'

'Dammit! Why wouldn't he tell us? We were all at Gundamurra for Christmas.'

'If Patrick thought it was the last one for him, he wouldn't have wanted to spoil it.'

'But…' Johnny lifted his hands in helpless frustration.

'Want to know what Mitch thinks?'

He waved a go-ahead, completely beyond imagining what had motivated such an extraordinary step.

'Patrick elected you to save Gundamurra. It's highly unlikely that Megan can do it by herself. The way things are going with the drought, she won't be able to service the mortgage. And it was you who always thought of it as home. Not me. Not Mitch. You.'

Johnny frowned. 'Mitch had a home with his mother and sister, but I thought you…' He searched Ric's eyes.

A very direct gaze accompanied his reply. 'You needed it more than I did, Johnny. And you can't deny it touches something in your soul. It comes out in your songs.'

Need…yes. There was so much hype and superficial crap in the career he had chosen, so much touring to make his success stick, it was the thought of Gundamurra that kept him sane, grounded, and going back there always put his world in perspective again—what was real, what wasn't.

'It won't be the same without Patrick.' Grief squeezed his heart. '*He* was the soul of Gundamurra.'

'You're forgetting Megan.'

Megan.

His mind shied away from thinking of her right now. Already he could see those stormy grey eyes hating him for being given half of *her place*, wishing he'd never set foot on Gundamurra, let alone have any claim on it.

'Patrick forgot his other daughters, Jessie and Emily,' he said, tearing his mind off the one daughter who'd become such a nagging thorn in his side.

'They've both made their lives away from Gundamurra and Patrick financed their ambitions,' Ric reminded him. 'I think they'll feel they've had their share. Jessie has her medical degree and the women's clinic she wanted at Alice Springs. Emily has her helicopter business at Cairns. The money to set them up was taken out of Gundamurra, probably contributing to the current debt. They can't be unaware of that.'

True enough, Johnny silently acknowledged, yet the family home was the family home. Leaving them out and putting him in might very well stir a sense of injustice. He couldn't help but feel uncomfortable about this inheritance on many counts. On the other hand, *Patrick had wanted him there* and it was impossible to discount a decision which would not have been taken lightly.

'It's up to you and Megan to pull Gundamurra through this bad patch and revive it, Johnny,' Ric gravely assured him. 'Patrick got it right.' He sighed and softly added, 'He always got it right.'

It was some relief that Ric thought so.

Mitch, too, apparently.

But no way was Megan was going to accept it gracefully.

Jessie and Emily might not, either, though Ric was right about their interests lying elsewhere and Patrick had put large investments behind their chosen careers. Besides which, both of them were married to men who shared those interests, Jessie's husband being a doctor for the Royal Doctor Flying Service, and Emily's husband a fellow helicopter pilot.

Only Megan was unmarried.

Not surprising with her bristling form of feminism, Johnny thought, wishing she'd stayed in the sweetly amenable little sister mould that he'd always found so engaging. *That* much younger Megan had never minded him stepping in and helping.

The flight steward came and took their glasses. The plane was about to take off. Johnny leaned back in his seat, closed his eyes and tried to relax. Fourteen hours to Sydney. Then the flight to Gundamurra in the far north west of New South Wales...the outback.

He felt the pull of it in his mind...the vast, seemingly empty land, wide-open space, searingly blue sky. It had a rhythm all its own—one that always felt good. The only jarring note was Megan standing in the middle of it, waiting for him, furiously frustrated because she had to share Gundamurra with *him*.

Had Patrick got it right?

The financial part, yes. Johnny could pour millions

into Gundamurra without a pang of personal loss. Mortgage gone with a simple transfer of money. Plus all the investment Megan needed to maintain the sheep station, eventually making it into a thriving concern again. But she certainly wouldn't welcome him into the life there. Over the past few years, her eyes had been branding him as an unwanted intruder, wanting him out.

But I'm in, Johnny thought on a surge of grim determination to keep what Patrick had granted him, regardless of Megan's reaction to it. He was co-owner. That gave him the right to be at Gundamurra whenever he wanted to and Megan would just have to stomach having him as her helpmate. Maybe, given time, he could whittle away whatever prejudice she had against him.

The leaden weight of grief eased as a strong sense of purpose grew. The outback was primitive—man against nature—a constant challenge that had to be won, just to survive, let alone prosper.

Above all else, Johnny was a survivor.

He wanted this challenge. Maybe he needed it. So come what might, he was going to hold his ground on Gundamurra. Patrick had entrusted it to him.

CHAPTER TWO

MEGAN finished doing her morning rounds, ensuring her work orders were being followed, checking for any problems, chatting to the families who still lived on the station, subtly assuring them that the status quo was not about to change. They were to carry on as usual.

She should have felt relieved that the sombre mood hanging over everyone for the past few days had lifted this morning, but the reason for it was a major irritant. *Johnny had arrived.* Never mind that Ric Donato and Mitch Tyler were also here. It was Johnny who put smiles on everyone's faces. Just the thought of him was enough to do it.

Charm…

It was as natural to him as breathing.

And it always reminded her what a hopelessly naive little fool she'd been to see it as something else when applied to her. There was no differentiation. He ladled it out to one and all—his trademark in the pop world where he was a big star, a master of light entertainment. It meant nothing. Absolutely nothing.

Having finally recognised that, she'd tried to bury the hurt of it and move on. It would have helped if he'd gone completely out of her life—out of sight, out of mind—but he kept coming back, making her feel bad about herself because it was stupid, stupid, stupid to still feel attracted to him. His interests lay elsewhere, wrapped up with his glittering successes overseas. Their lives did not mix. Never would.

Why hadn't her father seen that?

Why?

Had he only thought of the money needed—choosing the one person who could probably shed a few million dollars without even noticing it was gone?

Money as meaningless as charm.

Megan grimly determined to accept only what she absolutely had to in order to keep Gundamurra running. There was no avoiding confronting Johnny Ellis over what was to be done. He was here now, having come yesterday with Ric, flying his own plane in as he always did.

No doubt Mitch had told him about the will. Though even without that pressing business, he wouldn't have stayed away, not from her father's funeral. She could only hope that having started a new career in movies, he might be content to be an absent shareholder in Gundamurra. After all, her father was gone. No more *mentoring* readily available from Patrick Maguire.

As she walked back to the homestead, tears blurred her eyes. She didn't want to feel betrayed by what her father had done, yet the grief of losing him was so much harder to bear because he'd left her in this intolerable position of having to accept Johnny Ellis as co-owner of Gundamurra.

Her shock at the terms of the will had been followed by a wild surge of rebellion, a violent need to fight it. She'd argued fiercely with her sisters, but Jessie's and Emily's flat refusal to go against their father's decision left her without any support from them in a legal action to have it overturned.

In sheer desperation she'd broached the issue with Mitch Tyler, putting to him that Johnny might well have unfairly influenced her father. After all, she'd argued bitterly, he wasn't known as Johnny *Charm* for nothing.

Those laser-blue eyes of Mitch's had cut her down for even suggesting it, and his subsequent words had shamed her. 'Is that worthy of your father, Megan?'

He'd waited for her answer.

When she'd maintained a stubborn silence, squirming inside at the pertinent criticism of her viewpoint, Mitch had flatly stated, 'If you want to dishonour his will, I'm not your man. I'm here on Patrick's behalf, to help facilitate what *he* wanted. It's the very least I owe him for all he did for me.'

His high-minded integrity had goaded her into trying to bring it down a peg or two, force out some human weakness in him, make him empathise with what she was feeling. 'Why Johnny? My father took you in, too. And Ric. The three of you stayed in his life. Don't you feel slighted that he passed you over for…for a pop-star?'

It wouldn't have been so…difficult…having to share the property with either of his other *boys*. And there was no denying she needed help in these current circumstances. Ric would have dealt delicately with the problems, caring about her feelings. Mitch would have handled her needs from the city with efficiency and absolute integrity. But Johnny Ellis…whose whole life was about playing to an audience who loved him?

Mitch's straight black brows had beetled down. 'You don't understand your father's choice?'

'Do you?' she'd challenged.

'Yes. So does Ric. I think you need to talk to Johnny before taking any hostile step, Megan. You might not ever appreciate where he's come from, but...'

'I know what he is now,' she'd snapped.

'You've just pasted a label on the man which I know to be very superficial, Megan. Johnny has not yet reached the fulfilment of the person he is. I think...' He'd paused, his gravity giving way to a gleam of whimsical irony. 'Did Patrick teach you to play chess?'

'Yes. We played sometimes.'

'He always favoured a knight attack.'

'What has that got to do with anything?'

'It was a strategy, Megan. Your father thought out his strategies very carefully. Don't devalue the thought he put into his will when you talk to Johnny. Remember that Gundamurra was Patrick's life, as well as yours, and he knew how to share it.'

The sting of those words still hurt. She wasn't mean-hearted. She hadn't felt jealous of her father's pride in his three bad boys who'd made good. Nor of his affection for them.

She just didn't want Johnny Ellis constantly trampling through her life. She wished he'd married one of the gorgeous women he mixed with in his star-studded world so he wasn't free to drop in on her world whenever he liked.

At least, after the funeral, he'd have to go back to his cowboy movie. Hopefully he'd ride off into the sunset—anywhere else but here! She didn't begrudge him the fulfilment he was still looking for, as long as he stayed away and left her free to hold the reins at Gundamurra.

Maybe he could be persuaded to do just that.

With this purpose burning in her mind, Megan headed for the homestead kitchen. If Johnny was not still sleeping after his long trip from the U.S., he'd be there, being fed by Evelyn who'd be fussing over him with sickening adoration.

The housekeeper had been with the Maguire family all her life, born on the sheep station, and trained by Megan's mother to run the household with meticulous efficiency, just as she herself always had before cancer had taken her life. Everyone loved and respected Evelyn, but her attitude towards Johnny Ellis—as though the sun shone out of him—grated terribly on Megan.

It was bad enough that she never tired of listening to his songs, playing them over and over again. No doubt she'd be cooking up all his favourite foods, regardless of the current strict budget. Megan tried not to feel too critical of this indulgence as she opened the kitchen door…and came to an embarrassed halt, finding the highly dependable housekeeper weeping on Johnny Ellis's big, broad shoulder, his cheek rubbing the top of her head, one brawny arm holding her while the other was engaged in delivering soothing pats on her back.

It was instantly clear that the grief Evelyn had held in the past few days had suddenly overflowed and Johnny was comforting her. Megan stood rooted to the spot, realising that she and her sisters, wrapped in their own loss, had taken Evelyn's services to them for granted, not really considering that she, too, might feel devastated by their father's sudden death. It was Johnny who was giving her what she needed, sympathetic understanding and a shoulder to cry on.

What I need, too.

A painful loneliness stabbed through Megan's heart. Jessie and Emily had their husbands. Ric and Mitch had their wives. With her father gone, she had no-one to hold her, soothe her pain. And the sight of Johnny Ellis embracing Evelyn made it worse.

It wasn't fair that he looked like a strong, steady rock to lean on. His life was all about *image,* Megan fiercely told herself. Her gaze fixed scornfully on his riding boots—still playing the cowboy role—then noted how the denim of his jeans was tightly stretched around his powerful thighs, showing off how solidly built he was.

No doubt his female fans swooned over his macho sexiness, imagining his private parts were the ultimate in virility. Megan wondered just how many women didn't have to imagine, having known him intimately. Did he have a different one every night? Two or three a day?

It would have to be so easy for him, a mere crook of the finger. His star status would assure him of groupies everywhere. Though strictly on a male appeal level, he had the lot anyway; impressive physique, a very masculine face accentuated by a squarish jawline, a strong, almost triangular nose with its flaring nostrils, wickedly twinkling greenish eyes which were quite strikingly complemented by tanned skin and toffee-coloured hair, and, of course, the wide mouthful of white teeth that flashed winning smiles everywhere, not to mention the million-dollar voice.

Which suddenly crooned, 'I think this is the time for me to make *you* a cup of tea, Evelyn.'

The weeping had stopped.

With a choked little laugh, Evelyn lifted her head. 'No…no…' she said chidingly, reaching up to pat his cheek as he gently released her from his embrace. 'Thank you for letting me unburden my sorrows, but don't be taking away my pleasures now. You sit yourself down and let me get busy.'

Megan hadn't gathered wits enough to effect a swift retreat before the two of them moved apart and Johnny's swinging gaze caught her in the open door-way. Her stomach lurched as their eyes locked and she felt the sympathy he'd given to Evelyn being transmitted to her. She didn't want it from him. Didn't need anything from *him*. And be damned if she'd cry on his shoulder!

'Megan…come on in,' he invited, his hand beckoning her forward, taking charge, assuming control!

Not of me! Never! Megan silently and savagely vowed.

'Evelyn was just telling me about your fa-ther…how he'd been clutching your mother's pho-tograph from the bedside table in his hand when you found him,' he went on softly, sadly. 'I guess—'

'Yes.' She cut him off, feeling tears welling up again. 'I hope he's with my mother now. He missed her very much.' Fighting her way out of a storm of emotion, she waspishly added, 'I wonder if you'll ever know that kind of love, Johnny?'

His face tightened as though she had slapped him.

Evelyn gave a shocked gasp.

Acutely aware that the personal remark had slipped out of her previous thoughts and was totally inexcusable, Megan almost bit her tongue in chagrin. She had to deal with this man. That was best done by keeping as much *impersonal* distance from him as possible.

'I think finding that kind of love is rather rare in today's world,' Johnny answered in a measured tone.

'Especially yours,' flew out of her mouth before she could stop it.

'Miss Megan…'

Evelyn's reproof faded into a heavy sigh.

Megan gritted her teeth, refusing to take back what she believed. She glared defiance at the man who'd probably slept with thousands of women without giving any one of them any serious commitment. Her words had clearly struck a nerve and she took fierce satisfaction in the way his eyes glittered at her. No sympathy now.

'Rare in your world, too, Megan,' he countered, using his voice like a silky whip. 'Unless you've met the man of your dreams since Christmas.'

'Too busy,' she loftily retorted.

'Which reminds me…'

'We need to talk,' she leapt in before he could take charge of their *business* meeting. 'When you've finished your breakfast, perhaps you wouldn't mind coming to the office.'

'Whatever suits you,' he returned obligingly.

'That will be most appropriate. You'll find me there.'

She quickly closed the door and strode outside, marching off a mountain of turbulent energy as she headed for the front entrance of the homestead and the steps leading up to the verandah which skirted the huge house—a verandah that welcomed people out of the sun that could too often be pitiless in the Australian Outback.

She hadn't welcomed Johnny Ellis.

Couldn't welcome him.

Having reached the top of the steps she turned, her gaze skating around all the outbuildings that made Gundamurra look like a small township from the air; the big maintenance and shearing sheds, the prize rams' enclosure attached to the lab, the cottages for the long-term staff, the bunkhouse for jackaroos, the cook's quarters, the supplies store, the schoolhouse.

She was twenty-eight years old and this was her life—the life she'd chosen—the life she loved.

She didn't *need* a man.

Certainly not a man who peddled charm.

What she needed was this whole area to be an oasis of green again. Even the foliage on the pepper trees looked brown, coated with dust. All the land to the horizon was brown, and above it the sky was a blaze of blue, no clouds, no chance of rain.

If only the Big Wet had come this year, breaking the drought, her father might not have decided to write that will, making Johnny Ellis a permanent fixture in her life. The pressing question now was... how was she going to pry him out of it? Or at least, minimise his presence to next to nothing.

He didn't belong here.

With this thought firmly entrenched in her mind,

Megan went inside, passing through the great hall that bisected this section of the homestead, moving onto the verandah that skirted the inner quadrangle, heading straight for her father's office.

Once there, she found herself drawn to the chess table by the window, remembering what Mitch had said, that her father thought through his strategies very carefully. The black and white pieces were set up ready to play, which had to mean his last game with Mitch—played by e-mail—had been completed.

Game over, she thought, and on a deep wave of sadness, laid the black king down. She stared at the white knight, fretting further over why her father had thought Johnny Ellis was the right man to ride in to the rescue, then gave up on trying to figure it out and moved on to sit in the large leather chair behind the desk.

It was a big chair made for a big man. Physically she didn't fit it, never would, but at least her father had granted her the right to sit here in his place, and no way in the world was she going to let Johnny Ellis occupy it while they talked.

He was ten years her senior but that didn't give him any authority over her or what was to be decided in this room. It was she who owned fifty-one percent of Gundamurra…she who had the whip hand…and all the millions he'd made as a pop-star could not change that!

CHAPTER THREE

DEAL kindly with her...

Ric's admonition was playing through Johnny's mind as he approached Patrick's office, but Megan's attitude towards him made it damned difficult to keep it fixed there. Icy politeness from her last night and the least possible amount of contact. This morning, rejecting his sympathy point-blank, actually turning it into one of her snide hits on him, not even caring that Evelyn heard it, too.

All the same, he shouldn't have let himself be goaded into hitting back. Especially about the lack of any special love in her life. That was a low blow, especially when she'd just lost her father. Johnny grimaced over the insensitive lapse in his control. He had to do better in this meeting, not let Megan get under his skin. He was older than she was, had more people skills. It was up to him to...*deal kindly with her.*

At least he didn't have to worry about Jessie's and Emily's feelings. The two older sisters had welcomed him warmly last night, making it clear that their only concern was Megan's future on Gundamurra. The situation on the sheep station was grim. Like Patrick, they were counting on him to ensure there was a future here for her.

And he'd do it.

Even against Megan's prickly opposition he'd do it.

Though he hoped she'd be reasonable.

The situation demanded she be reasonable.

He paused at the office door, took a deep, calming breath, gave a courtesy knock to warn of his imminent entry, allowed Megan a few seconds to get her mind into appropriate gear, then moved in with every intention of being at his diplomatic best.

But he wasn't prepared for the scene Megan had set and his sense of rightness was instantly jolted. She was sitting in Patrick's chair, taking Patrick's place before he was even buried. It was too soon. It was...

Johnny checked himself, took stock of the woman he had to deal with.

The defiance in her eyes could mean she was making a statement by taking her father's chair—a statement of empowerment that she might feel a need for in this situation. And being seated there put the desk between them, a decisive distance that possibly suggested she was feeling vulnerable about having to deal with him.

They were the kindest thoughts Johnny could come up with.

'Megan,' he acknowledged softly, nodding for her to take the lead in this meeting.

'It was good of you to come, Johnny...'

Which was a pleasant enough greeting until she added, '...being in the middle of shooting your first movie.'

Kind thoughts flew out the window. He eyeballed

her in furious challenge, every muscle in his body taut with aggression at this belittling of his feelings for her father. Patrick had been the most important person in his life and Megan could not be ignorant of how very much their relationship had meant to him.

Not one word passed his lips, but the force of his anger obviously got through to her. A tide of heat burned up her neck and scorched her cheeks, lighting up the freckles that added a cuteness to her pert little nose. Except Johnny wasn't thinking *cute* right now. He was thinking *little*. No way was she big enough to take over from her father, not in any sense.

She gestured to the chairs at the chess table, her gaze shifting from his. 'Please take a seat.' The words were husky, as though she was pushing them through a very tight throat.

Satisfied that he'd wrung some shame from her, Johnny stepped over to the chess table to move Mitch's chair—not Patrick's—into a face-to-face position with Megan. The fallen black king caught his eye. What was this? The king is dead...long live the queen?

Johnny pulled himself up again. Mitch might have laid the chess piece down—a symbol of Patrick resting in peace. Leaping to hasty and possibly false conclusions was not conducive to a fair meeting. He rolled the chair out from the table and closer to the desk, then sat down, telling himself to watch and listen, refrain from stirring any more hostility in Megan's mind. Though what he'd ever done to earn it was a total mystery to him.

He stared at her, waiting for her to start. The scarlet heat had receded from her face, leaving her skin pale and the freckles more prominent. She wore no make-up, hadn't done for years, though he remembered her experimenting with it in her teens. She'd been a happier person then, enjoying his company. They'd had fun together, laughing easily, chatting easily. Then she'd gone away to some agricultural college and something had changed her.

She could have been quite strikingly beautiful if she'd put her mind to it...good bones, big expressive eyes that could twinkle like silver or brood like storm clouds, a full-lipped mouth when it wasn't thinned with disapproval of him, and a glorious mane of red curls, currently pulled back into some tight clip at the back of her neck. A lovely long neck it was, too.

Apparently she didn't care how she looked. Being a woman was not her thing. When had she last worn a dress? A checked shirt and jeans was her usual garb, as it was today. Maybe she wanted to look like a man in them but she didn't.

As much as she might try to minimise her femininity, her figure was too curvaceous for anyone to mistake her for a male. In fact, her antagonism towards him over the past few years had made him acutely aware of her as a woman, especially when she turned her back on him, her taut cheeky bottom wagging her disdain of what he stood for in her eyes, stirring feelings in him that were entirely inappropriate, given she was Patrick's daughter.

Did she resent having been a daughter instead of a son?

Was that why she looked so sourly on him…because he had a similar physique to her father?

Johnny hadn't meant to speak first, yet the question that rose in his mind seemed imperative, at the very core of the situation that had to be settled between them. The words tumbled out, seeking the answer that might make sense of Megan Maguire's attitude towards him.

'What happened to the girl who used to like me?'

I grew up.

Megan wasn't about to give that answer, nor explain the milestones that had marked her passage to where she was now. She looked at Johnny Ellis, knowing he was thirty-eight, yet the years sat so easily on him, she could still see the sixteen-year-old boy who'd made up songs for her when she was just a little kid—songs that had generated dreams that were never going to come true for her.

The monumental crush she'd had on him in her teens had finally bitten the dust when he hadn't come home for her twenty-first birthday. She'd planned for him to see her as a woman, but her coming of age had obviously meant nothing to him. He'd stayed in the U.S., busy with his career, and no doubt involved with the kind of woman who shared his limelight. She was just Patrick Maguire's youngest daughter, someone he was nice to when it suited him to visit Gundamurra.

Facile charm.

Meaningless.

It was her father who'd drawn him back to

Gundamurra…her father who had given him almost half of it in his will, trapping her into this ridiculous and frustrating partnership with a man whose life was aimed at adding more stars to his celebrity status.

'Do you need everyone to like you, Johnny?' she lightly taunted, hoping he'd hightail it back to Hollywood where everybody probably fawned on him.

He shrugged, his eyes holding hers in challenge. 'Usually I know why not. Where you're concerned, I'm at a total loss, Megan. What have I done to you to warrant your dislike? Best spit it out now before we get into business together.'

'What reason could I have for disliking you, Johnny?' she countered. 'You've always been charming to me.' Which was absolutely true. 'As for doing business together,' she quickly ran on, 'I don't imagine you'll want to take an active part in running Gundamurra. You do have a movie to finish and probably many more in your pipeline.'

'No. Just the one. Which I'm committed to by contract,' he stated drily. 'Undoubtedly, people will wait to see how well I perform on screen before other offers come in.'

'Oh, I'm sure with your star quality—'

'Let's not speculate on a hypothetical future, Megan,' he cut in. 'We're here to discuss the far more immediate future of Gundamurra, are we not?' He cocked a challenging eyebrow at her. 'Can we be honest about that?'

She felt herself burning again. She'd thought a bit of flattery—pandering to the ego that stars of his magnitude had to have—would set the scene she wanted to play through with him. But his eyes were seeing straight through that ploy, mocking her attempt to manipulate what she saw as his push to be loved by more and more fans through the movies he could make.

'You need not be concerned about the running of Gundamurra, Johnny. I'll be doing that,' she stated with grim determination.

'I don't doubt you're capable of it, Megan, given enough resources to ride through the drought. That's where I come in.'

The lack of resources…there was no denying that, though there'd been no mismanagement. Her father had taken out the first big loan from the bank to finance Emily's helicopter business, before the drought started biting deep. Then to keep the sheep alive, keep paying wages, more loans…and wool prices had dropped. The mortgage now was so big, Megan didn't know how she could service it with no relief from the drought in sight. Even if it rained tomorrow, she'd need recovery time.

A rescue package had to be accepted from Johnny Ellis if she was to keep Gundamurra. Except it wasn't entirely hers to keep. It was his, too. And she still didn't know how he wanted to work their partnership. He'd just denied her any sense of security about him going away and staying away.

'We need an injection of funds,' she admitted flatly.

He nodded. 'I'll wipe out the mortgage today, get the bank off your back.'

Just like that! Megan instantly bridled at how easy

it was for him while she had sweated over every dollar being spent. 'No, you won't!' The denial exploded from a deep well of pride.

He frowned. 'I have the funds, Megan.'

'I don't want to owe you fifty-one percent of the mortgage.' She glared defiantly at him. 'If you pay off forty-nine percent of it, I can get another loan from the bank which could see me through...'

'Why put yourself through that worry when you don't have to?' he argued, waving an impatient dismissal of her counterproposal.

'Because I won't take your charity,' she shot back at him.

'Charity?'

He rose from his chair, glaring down at her from his formidable height, a big man, as big as her father had been, emanating a power that wanted to blast her point of view to smithereens. He raised a clenched fist, shaking it as he spoke with more passion than she'd ever heard from Johnny Charm.

'I owe *my life* to this place. I don't want to see it go under. I didn't like seeing it struggle to survive. I offered your father...'

He closed his mouth into a tightly compressed line, shutting down on the vehement flow of emotion.

What had he offered her father, Megan thought wildly. What? Had it influenced the terms of the will?

Johnny stepped forward, pressed his hands on the desk, leaning forward, his eyes firing bullets at her. 'I now have the right to do what I'm going to do. Patrick gave me the right.'

'He didn't give you the right to interfere with my

share,' she fired back, refusing to be intimidated into being indebted to him.

'You can pay me back when you can, Megan. If you must. But the bank is not going to have any claim on Gundamurra.'

'Even if I let you do that, I'll have to borrow again to keep going,' she pointed out, mocking his ignorance of what had to be done.

'No. I'll set up an account for you to draw from,' came the swift reply. He was all primed to fix everything with his money.

Her jaw set stubbornly. 'I won't accept that.'

'You don't know how long this drought will last.'

'I'll manage it my way.'

Frustration boiled through Johnny. Megan would put Gundamurra at risk again and there was no need for it. He wanted to pick her up and shake some sense into her, but there was steel in the grey eyes so fiercely defying him—Patrick's eyes—and he knew he had to find another way of convincing her to use the money he could provide.

He straightened up, turned away, walked over to the window, stared out at the one patch of green left on Gundamurra—the homestead quadrangle. Not all the millions of dollars he had available could turn the rest of the vast sheep station green. Only rain could do that. Lots of rain.

However, an unencumbered supply of funds could pay for feed to be trucked in. It could pay wages. It could make life absolutely secure for everyone here, bring back those who'd had to leave. They could comfortably wait out the drought, be ready for the good times to come again.

'Would you prefer me to buy you out, Megan?' he tossed at her with little hope.

'No,' came the firm and predictable reply. Her eyes said she'd have to be forcibly dragged off Gundamurra, no letting it go of her own free will.

He shrugged. 'I thought, since you dislike having to deal with me so much…'

'You overstepped the line, Johnny,' she informed him rigidly. 'By all means wipe out your share of the mortgage. That's your right.'

'Fine!' he snapped. 'Do you want to draw a line through Gundamurra, divide it up so I can pour whatever funds I like into salvaging my forty-nine percent of it?'

Treat her kindly…

Maybe there was truth in the old adage that one had to be cruel to be kind.

Her jaw clenched. 'My father wouldn't have wanted that,' she grated out.

'Have you stopped to think of what your father did want…instead of what *you* want?'

'He didn't accept your money while he was alive.'

He pounced on that statement, inflamed by her antagonism towards him. 'Because *you* argued against it?'

'No. I didn't know about any offer. You just mentioned it yourself, Johnny.'

Her eyes were clearly weighing its effect on Patrick's will. He blasted her calculation by informing her, 'Ric and Mitch offered help, too. All three of us, Megan.'

Confusion looked back at him. 'Then why choose *you?*'

It was eating at her. 'Would Ric or Mitch have been more acceptable to you?' he tested, wanting to know if his friends were equally unwelcome in her life.

'That's not the question,' she snapped evasively.

'I think it's pertinent. Why not me?' he challenged.

Intriguing to watch the flush come again, sweeping into her cheeks with blazing heat. She dropped her gaze and fiercely claimed, 'I can manage on my own. With the mortgage reduced, I can...'

'What if you can't? Why risk it?' He paused, sure now in his own mind that *he* was the problem. 'Is your dislike of me so great that you can't bear to let me help?'

'I don't dislike you! It's just not right!' she burst out, banging her own hands on the desk as she leaned forward to deliver this declaration with vehemence.

'Then what would make it right for you, Megan?'

The storm of feeling in her eyes gave way to a dull bleakness. Johnny read the answer in her mind—*Nothing.* Was she looking down a black pit, too, with her father dead?

'I don't know. I don't know,' she muttered, shaking her head over the wretched admission and sagging back in the chair, shoulders slumped in defeat.

She looked so miserable, for the second time this morning, Johnny felt the urge to pick her up, but not to shake her, to wrap her in a comforting embrace and promise her he would make everything better. He remembered doing that when she was a little kid.

She'd been running to tell him something and fallen over, scraping her knees—such a sweet little girl, clinging to him, trusting him to make the hurt go away.

He'd loved that little girl.

Patrick's youngest daughter.

Maybe that was what Patrick's will was about… taking care of Megan. But how was he to do it?

His gaze dropped to the chess table.

What was the phrase used where no-one could win?

Stalemate.

He had to start again, adopt a strategy that would get past Megan's pride. If she really didn't dislike him, there had to be other factors involved in her attitude towards him, perhaps a love affair gone wrong when she'd been at that agricultural college, seeding some drive to prove herself completely independent, basing her whole future on taking over from her father. If she was stuck in that groove, how could he ease her out of it?

Not by anything she perceived as charity.

Slowly, accompanied by a weird sense of many factors pushing it, an idea came to him.

It was totally wild. Absurdly quixotic. Yet the more he thought about it the more it appealed to him. On many levels. Especially the prospect of wearing down Megan's resistance to it, winning her over.

Though that mission could well prove impossible.

Still, something was needed to break this hopeless impasse and the shock of his offer might open Megan up more, give him an understanding of how she viewed him. He certainly had nothing to lose by putting it on the table. In heaping more scorn on him, she would have to give reasons for it, reasons he could work on.

He pasted an ironic little smile on his mouth and aimed it at her. 'You know, Megan, you'd have the right to all I could provide…if you married me.'

CHAPTER FOUR

MARRY him...

Megan felt her jaw drop in sheer shock.

Incredulity blanked her mind for several seconds.

Her heart rocketed around her chest in some stupid manic excitement until the words that had preceded Johnny's proposal hit home, firing up a surge of anger that lifted her right out of her father's chair to hurl a furious rejection at him.

'You think I'd marry you for your money?'

She didn't wait for a reply, so totally incensed by the suggestion, she flew straight into attack. 'How dare you lump me with the kind of women who hang off you for what you can give them?' Her arms scissored a dismissal of absolute disgust. 'Which just goes to prove how tainted your thinking is by the life you lead. Buy a woman here. Buy a woman there. Have one in every port of call.'

Her mocking hands landed on her hips, planting themselves there in a belligerent flaunting of her own femininity which wasn't for sale. 'Well, not at Gundamurra. Not even if I was reduced to eating dirt would I join that queue for your favours.'

He had the gall to look amused, his eyes twinkling unholy mischief at her as he observed, 'So, you see me as some indiscriminate sex machine, churning through women at a rate of knots, probably not even remembering their names.'

She glared back at him, wishing she hadn't let her tongue loose on this theme.

He strolled towards her, gesturing an open invitation to continue. 'I'd like to hear what evidence you have that formed this picture of me.'

'Oh, don't pretend there haven't been swarms of groupies after you,' she snapped, folding her arms across her chest to contain herself against the strength of his attraction as he came at her. 'Anyone in a sweet shop gets tempted to taste,' she fired to pull him up short.

It didn't so much as make him pause. He hitched himself onto the other side of her father's desk, bringing his eye level down to a very direct line with hers, holding her gaze with a mocking intensity that squeezed her heart, making it thump in painful protest.

'Did you ever make these comments about me to your father, Megan?'

'No. Why would I? I'm sure he understood where you were at, Johnny,' she returned with acid emphasis.

'Yes, he did. He took the time to understand exactly where I was at when I was sixteen.'

'Sixteen.' She rolled her eyes. 'You weren't a huge star then.'

'No. I was a street-kid, whose only knowledge of how life worked was firmly planted in being used and using back, perpetuating a system of abuse.'

She frowned, not relating to this picture at all. 'I remember you as always being a happy person.'

He shrugged. 'I'd learnt that a smile could ward

off many evils, as well as hide what no-one wants to know about.'

'Huh!' she pounced. 'I knew the legendary charm was all a pose.'

The satisfaction in her voice drew a quizzical look from him. 'It began as a survival tactic. But now I like to make people feel good. Is that so wrong to you?'

'It's deceptive.'

'Deceptive?' he repeated critically, goading her into ignoring a defensive caution.

'It draws people into thinking they're special to you and they're not. They don't really touch your life at all.'

'Every person is special, Megan.' His eyes bored into hers, rattling her deep box of resentments as his voice gathered an emotional vehemence. 'Didn't your father teach you that? Didn't your father show, by example, that he believed it? And lived by it?'

His gaze moved to the chair she had vacated in her anger, and the look on his face—the raw anguish of wanting to see her father there and knowing he never could be again—made her realise how offensive it had been to him to find her sitting in it, assuming a place that was irreplaceable in his mind.

He nodded to the chair. 'Patrick taught me to value my own individuality. He explained why I shouldn't let myself be used, why I shouldn't accept any more abuse, how allowing it diminished the person I could be, and if I held on to a strong belief in the music I personally loved and trod my own path, I could climb out of the belittling pattern of use and abuse which had been my life for as long as I could remember.'

Abuse… She hadn't thought about his life before he came to Gundamurra. Mitch had said something about her not appreciating where Johnny had come from. Had he suffered a traumatic childhood? But that was so long ago. He'd become so successful, it couldn't still shadow his life…could it?

He turned a fierce glittery look back to her. 'So I am who I am, Megan. I don't have to belittle anyone else to make myself bigger. I don't abuse the position I have by taking what is offered to me for all the wrong reasons. Far from being *tempted by the sweet shop,* I feel sorry for the people who populate it because they have never learnt to value themselves. They think if they get a piece of me, it will make their lives better. But it won't. Any change for the better has to come from within.'

It was an impressive speech, forcing her to reassess how she'd painted his life in her mind. Okay, he'd stepped away from continuing a cycle of abuse. Yes, she could see her father's hand in that. But rejecting every attractive 'freebie' that came his way?

'I don't screw my fans, Megan,' he went on, obviously reading the doubt in her eyes. 'But they do touch my life and I try to touch theirs through the lyrics of my songs, which carry the same set of values that your father taught me. Patrick knew that. I don't know why you think otherwise.'

Oh, great! Now it was Saint Johnny, as well as the king of charm. 'You're a man!' she flashed at him, unable to swallow such a pinnacle of nobility. 'As for your songs, isn't it simply clever commercialism to tap into the dreams people nurse for themselves? That's street smart, Johnny.'

His eyes raked her derisively. 'And you want to put me back in the gutter where I belong. Is that it, Megan?'

'No. You're perfectly welcome to the brilliant heights of Hollywood.'

'As long as I leave Gundamurra to you. To an embittered woman who'd rather let it die than accept the help of *a man.*'

The sudden counterattack shocked her into hot denial. 'I am not an embittered woman!'

'What happened to you? Did you feel *used* by a man? Did he only want sex from you instead of the whole package?'

'That's none of your business!'

'Oh, yes, it is, Megan. You've made it my business by the way you treat me, giving me the low-life status of a rutting animal that doesn't care what body he uses for sexual release.'

'Okay! So you don't do that,' she granted, though some defence was called for. 'You can't blame me for thinking it. Pop-stars are notorious for taking what they can.'

'Except I don't have that reputation. Yet you lumped me with it anyway. Because I'm *a man?*'

'Because you're Johnny Charm,' she jeered, hating the way he was turning the tables on her, digging into her life. 'And you can't deny that draws a lot of women to you.'

'But not Megan Maguire,' he mocked. '*She* won't be one of the herd. *She'll* stand aloof and scorn his company.'

That was too close. Far too close. She lashed back.

'What's the matter, Johnny? You can't stand not having everyone worship you?'

He bored in again. 'Why have you been so ready and willing to give me feet of clay, Megan? I haven't used you or abused you. Did the guy you fell for at agricultural college turn out to be a womaniser, charming his way into one bed after another?'

'Why haven't you married if you're not a womaniser yourself?' she retorted, fighting for any foothold that would exonerate her attitude.

He grimaced, his expression changing to an inner musing. 'There wasn't anyone I could bring here. Not one in all these years.' He shook his head, shifted off the desk, a wry look on his face as he turned away from her and strolled back towards the chess table. 'Ric had no hesitation in bringing Lara here...'

Megan couldn't see the relevance. Lara had needed a safe refuge. What better place than an outback sheep station?

'...Mitch brought Kathryn...'

He picked up the black king she had laid down on the chess table, his thumb running over the carved wood as though he wished he could bring it to life. Was he remembering that her father had played chess with Kathryn, as well as Mitch?

'They understood about Patrick. About Gundamurra,' he went on, his voice dropping to the soft deep timbre that invariably stirred an emotional response in his songs. 'They could take it on board, accept it, appreciate it, live with it.'

But they didn't live here, Megan corrected in her mind. Their lives were centred in the city.

He placed the king back on the chess table, standing it upright, nodding to it as though in respect, then swinging around to face her with a rueful little smile. 'The companions I've had from time to time were happy to share Johnny Charm's life, but they wouldn't have wanted Johnny Ellis.'

She shook her head in confusion. 'You've lost me.'

'Oh, I lost you a long time ago, Megan,' he drawled, cocking his head to one side as he looked her over in a distant, objective appraisal. 'I think you lost yourself, as well. You do your utmost to deny that you're a woman, neutering your femininity in men's clothes, scraping back your hair...'

'That's purely practical for the work I do,' she defended hotly.

His gaze dropped to her folded arms. 'Whole body language telegraphing *keep away*. That guy at college sure must have done a number on you. I would have thought Patrick's daughter would have had guts enough not to be a victim, to know her own worth...'

'I do, dammit!' She flung out her arms in defiance of his reading. 'Which is why I won't be bought with a marriage proposal from you!'

'That was more a provocative thought than a proposal, Megan.' His mouth curled in sardonic humour. 'And it did provoke quite a lot, didn't it?'

She burned over how much she had revealed. He hadn't even been serious. He'd set a trap and she'd leapt right into it. The urge to return to her father's chair, regain the authority she needed, had her swinging towards it, but the realisation hit her that Johnny would despise her if she claimed that seat again in these current circumstances.

Somehow she had to snatch some initiative. Reversing direction, she rounded the desk, placing herself against the front of it, hands propped on the edge, adopting a commanding though relaxed position, and tossed out the only thing she could think of to put Johnny Ellis on his back foot.

'What if I'd said I *would* marry you?'

He had the nerve to grin at her, a grin she wished she could smack right off his face. Topping that irritation came his totally rocking reply, 'Then we could very well be planning a wedding.'

He didn't mean it. Of course, he didn't mean it! He was watching her, watching for a chink in her armour through which he could draw more blood. She tossed her head disdainfully and scoffed, 'You've got to be joking.'

'Am I? It wasn't so long ago that marriage was all about consolidating property.' His eyes seemed to sizzle a challenge at her as he added, '*And* having heirs to it.'

Her stomach contracted at the thought of Johnny Ellis fathering her children. Her mind savagely denied any desire for a sexual connection with him and snatched at a pointedly mocking reply. 'We don't live in feudal times anymore and I would hate being stuck in a loveless marriage while my husband gallivanted around the world doing his thing.'

His eyebrows lifted in equally mocking surprise. 'I thought you'd settled on Gundamurra as the love of your life. Why would you care what your husband did as long as he provided you with a future here?'

He was twisting everything around to make the unacceptable sound reasonable. She had to end this ridiculous conversation. 'I'll make my own future,' she stated emphatically.

'Which you'll have to share with me, anyway,' he reminded her.

'Not...intimately!'

'It could be productive.'

'Oh, stop it, Johnny!' she burst out in frustration, pushing off the front of the desk and almost folding her arms again, stopping herself by clenching her hands at her sides and flaming at him, 'Don't play this stupid game with me!'

He instantly sobered. 'Not so stupid, Megan. It uncovered a prejudice you've been nursing for years. An unjust prejudice. I hope you'll now lay it aside so we can be friends.'

She didn't want to be *friends* with him. She wanted...

'Friends with a common purpose,' he went on. 'To save Gundamurra. It doesn't matter where I'm coming from. It doesn't matter where you're coming from. We both care about this place. So just let it be, Megan. I supply the money. You put it to good use. It's as simple as that. And what your father wanted.'

She looked at Johnny Ellis and saw a mountain of unshakeable purpose.

He wasn't going to go away until she agreed.

Fighting him was futile.

Worse...it stirred up all she had to keep hidden from him.

Her father had ordained this.

Her father...

A huge lump of emotion blocked her throat. Tears pricked her eyes. She jerked into action, walking around the desk again, pausing by her father's chair, her hand sliding up the worn leather of the back rest, gripping the top of its wooden frame, wanting the strength that had been embodied in this chair to seep into her. She swallowed hard and forced out the words that had to be said.

'All right. You supply the money and I'll use it however it will best serve Gundamurra. If you'll go and get Mitch now, we'll sort out the necessary financial arrangements.'

'Megan…'

The soft caress of his voice shivered down her spine. 'Please…just go.'

She heard him heave a long sigh. 'I just wanted to say…I know you consider Gundamurra as your birthright and you see me as an intruder. But in a very real sense, I was reborn here. It's home to me, too. It always will be.'

Always…

A shudder ran through her. Every muscle in her body tensed as she heard him move, relaxing only when she heard the office door being opened and shut.

Gone.

But he'd be back.

And if this was home to him, even without her father here, he might always come back. He had every right to. He owned forty-nine percent of Gundamurra. There was no escape from sharing it with him.

What if she said she would marry him?

Would he really marry her...forsaking all others...till death do they part?

A pipedream.

A stupid, stupid pipedream!

The reality was he'd go off about his business whenever it suited him—a business *she* couldn't share because Gundamurra needed all her time and attention—and she'd be left wondering who *was* sharing his life away from her.

A great marriage that would be!

But if he was unfaithful to her, she could divorce him and maybe get his share of Gundamurra in the settlement.

Dear God! She was thinking like a bitch! A horrible, nasty bitch! All because... She closed her eyes and dredged up the real truth...the truth that had been festering behind all her responses to Johnny Ellis since she'd been old enough to acknowledge the deep down craving. She wanted him to love her. Love her as the one and only woman he wanted.

CHAPTER FIVE

IT HAD been a long tension-filled day for Johnny and he was glad when Mitch and Ric suggested a stroll down to the jackeroos' bunkhouse after dinner. The women were occupied, going through the funeral arrangements for the following day. Jessie's and Emily's husbands had retreated to the games room for a quiet game of billiards. Soon they would all go to bed, make it an early night, because tomorrow…was the last farewell.

It was a relief to be outside under the outback sky with its brilliant canopy of stars—a relief for it to be just the three of them for a while—old friends who'd forged an understanding that didn't need words. They'd come here for six months when they were sixteen, and here they were again, twenty-two years later, silently sharing memories that belonged only to them…and the man whose spirit they carried in their minds.

'Is Megan okay with you, Johnny?' Ric asked.

'She has accepted my financial help,' he answered.

'I told Ric the rescue package is in place,' Mitch put in. 'That's not what he's asking, Johnny.'

He heaved a rueful sigh. 'She's moved from hostile to passive neutral. I'm working on it, Ric. Given time…'

'You don't have much time,' came the quiet reminder.

'It's hard for Megan to see past my…other interests. But I think we broke some barriers today.'

'I'm worried about her,' Mitch said. 'She looked and sounded…defeated.'

Johnny frowned over the description, not liking it.

'Megan is Patrick's daughter. She'll fight her way up again.'

'Be good if you could make it to friends before you leave, Johnny,' Ric observed.

'I'm working on it,' he repeated.

'Problem is…she's so young,' Mitch commented.

'Not young for what she does here. She can handle it. I have no doubts on that score,' Johnny said with certainty.

'I meant…young…for understanding about you. You're a bit of a cowboy, Johnny. I hope you didn't ride too roughshod over her this morning.'

'Roughshod! Let me tell you, if I'm a cowboy, she's one hell of a prickly cactus.'

Ric laughed. 'Got under your skin, did she?'

More than Johnny was prepared to admit. 'I told you…I'm working on it.'

'Smooth it over,' Mitch advised. 'You're good at that.'

Except his *charm* didn't work with Megan.

Ric had the final word. 'Make friends with her.'

Friends…

Johnny was having severe problems with that concept.

Easy enough to say it as a pacifier—*friends with a common purpose*. It had been the safest thing to say to Megan in the circumstances. And he had to give her credit for trying to proceed on that basis.

She'd stopped her snide attacks on him, been amenable to the financial arrangements he and Mitch had set up—absolutely no argument there—and after lunch, she'd willingly laid out to him the most urgent problems to be dealt with at Gundamurra.

Yet there was a sick distance in her eyes, a dull flatness to her voice, and while Johnny could respect the consummate knowledge and experience she'd displayed where the running of the sheep station was concerned, he'd been constantly distracted by the urge to cosset and comfort her. Not as a child, either.

He'd found himself becoming more and more conscious of her as a woman, studying her mouth, her ears, the few little curly tendrils of hair that hadn't made it into the tight confinement of the clip at the back of her neck, the shape of her hands, the nervous mannerism she had of running her thumb over her fingerpads, making him want to wrap his own hand around hers and smooth away the fretting.

All the talk about sexual experience this morning had its influence, as well, stirring a host of tantalising thoughts, and urges that weren't so high-minded. Had she ever known real pleasure with a man, or had the guy—guys?—she'd known at college been the crass sort who cared only about their own satisfaction? He suspected she'd been tightly buttoned up for years and that wasn't right. He wanted to free her from those bad memories, make her stop wasting herself.

Or did he simply *want* her?

Certainly her fiery pride had stirred a caveman streak in him that itched to carry her off to bed, strip her of the clothes she wore to deny her sexuality, and force her to acknowledge she was a woman with needs that could be answered if she'd submit to letting it happen with him.

But she was dead against him as a man.

Much less a husband...

And there was no denying he had to get back to Arizona to finish the movie, leaving her in charge of Gundamurra. This was not the time to make any move on Megan. His top priority was to establish and reinforce a working relationship that benefited the drought-stricken sheep station. When he returned—and that was months away—she might look more kindly on him. It would be good to see warmth in her eyes. Oddly enough, he'd preferred the sparks of scorn to bleak grey.

The bunkhouse was empty—no jackaroos in residence. Gundamurra was operating with only permanent staff who lived in cottages on the property.

The three of them automatically headed for the bunks they had once occupied, flopping onto them, stretching out, remembering the fears and griefs and dreams they had shared in the darkness of long-ago nights.

They talked about Patrick, as only they could.

For Johnny, it reinforced all he felt about Gundamurra.

He made up his mind to take time out from his career once the movie was finished, come back and stay, find out if it held enough to keep him happy here. His life had moved a long way since he was sixteen. It had been quite a journey with many satisfying milestones, yet the tug of home had never been diminished.

And now Patrick had called him home.

His last will and testament.

Share Gundamurra with Megan.

Or should he give it up to her? Save it from bankruptcy, ensure it could continue running without any insurmountable disaster laying it completely to waste, then leave it to his daughter—a gift in return for the gift of life Patrick had held out to him.

What had been in Patrick's mind when he'd written that will?

Johnny felt honour-bound to get it right.

But what was right?

His mind was torn in many directions and he couldn't bring himself to talk them through with Ric and Mitch. The feelings he had about Megan were too private. And very possibly it would be wrong to act on them.

Eventually they left the bunkhouse, said goodnight to each other. Johnny felt a stab of envy as his old friends went off to bed where the women who loved them would be waiting—women who knew and understood all about them and loved who they were. He walked alone around the verandah that skirted the inner quadrangle of the four-winged homestead, stopped at the door to his bedroom, felt too restless to go inside.

He moved over to the verandah railing, leaning on it as he gazed out at the one square of lawn on Gundamurra that was still alive, watered by an underground bore, piped in especially to keep this grass green. Patrick's wife had insisted on it. She was happy to live in the outback, as long as she had one square of green to look at. Pepper trees had been planted at each corner of the quadrangle to provide shade for the bench seats placed under them.

This was where everyone on the station gathered on Christmas Eve, singing carols, making merry. Johnny usually led them in the singing, playing his guitar, sitting on that bench…

He jolted upright.

Someone was sitting there now.

Megan.

He knew it instinctively.

Megan alone…as he was.

He didn't stop to think she might want to be left to herself. His feet moved straight into action. The compulsion to close the distance between them pounded through Johnny's heart. She didn't have to be alone. He didn't want her to feel alone. Patrick had willed him to be here for her.

Megan's pulse rocketed into overdrive.

Johnny had seen her.

He was coming.

She'd meant to speak to him, had sat out here in the hope of catching him before he went to bed, yet courage had failed her when the opportunity had come. He'd been with Ric and Mitch, revisiting the bunkhouse, and she'd suddenly felt hopelessly young, having understood nothing of their backgrounds—how bad it had been for them—because she'd only been six years old when they'd first come to Gundamurra.

Maybe the age gap was too big for her ever to cross.

Stupid dreams…

Why couldn't she let them go?

'Mind if I join you, Megan?' His voice was soft and deep, seeming to carry the dark loneliness of the night.

She looked up. A big man. As big as her father. Broad shoulders. Ready and willing to carry the weight of Gundamurra on them. For her father. For her.

But *with* her? For the rest of their lives?

Her chest tightened up. She took a deep breath, fiercely told herself she had to be fair, and said, 'I'd like you to, Johnny.'

He settled on the seat beside her, leaning forward, his forearms resting on his thighs, hands linked between his knees. 'I miss him, too, Megan,' he said softly, 'though I guess your sense of loss encompasses much more, having been with your father every day, working with him…'

'Don't!' She swallowed hard to press back the swift welling of grief. 'I need to talk to you about…about something else,' she rushed out.

'Whatever you want,' he gruffly offered.

Want… He didn't have a clue what she *wanted* of him. Was it so hopeless? He hadn't married. Hadn't met anyone he felt right about bringing here. If she showed him she understood something of what he felt…though she didn't really. His pop-star life kept getting in the way.

He turned towards her, reached across and took her hand from her lap, wrapping his around it, holding it still. 'You'll wear your fingerprints out doing that,' he gently chided. 'Come on, Megan. Spit it out.

You had no hesitation in letting me have it straight between the eyes this morning.'

'But my aim was wrong, Johnny. I wanted to shoot you down in flames and…and I had it so screwed up…'

'It's okay,' he soothed.

'It's not okay!' she flared, not wanting to be *indulged*. 'Mitch told me I didn't know where you were coming from and I just brushed that aside because I didn't want to see…didn't want to know any good reason for Dad choosing *you*.'

'I'm sorry it was such a bad shock, on top of everything else.'

His thumb caressed her palm, sending warm tingles right up her arm. It was difficult to keep her mind focussed on what had to be said. All her defensive instincts were urging her to reject his touch, not let herself feel this treacherous thrill of pleasure in it. Yet if she stopped being negative, stopped fighting…

'I never asked Dad about you…' she blurted out, determined on at least clearing the air between them. '…about your life before you came here. You were just Johnny to me. Then later on you were Johnny, the star, making a big name for yourself.'

'All through your childhood and teen years, I liked the fact I was just Johnny to you, Megan. I would have liked it to stay that way. I had more than enough people only seeing me as a star,' he said drily.

She was glad he couldn't see the angst stirred by that statement. 'I'm sorry I took a…a bad view of you.'

Whether he sensed the angst, she didn't know, but

he instantly injected some humour into his tone, trying to lighten the conversation. 'Well, it was certainly a change from the usual reaction I got from
women. Brought me down to earth with a thump
every time I came back to Gundamurra.'

'Stop it, Johnny!' she cried in exasperation. 'I
don't want your charm. I'd rather know what's behind it.'

She sought his eyes but he looked away, his gaze
lifting to the stars in the sky. His hand started to
squeeze hers, then relaxed again, as though he was
very conscious of not transmitting tension. Yet she
sensed it was coiled inside him, wound tightly
around whatever it was he didn't want to reveal.

'When the three of you went off to the bunkhouse
tonight, I had a talk with Lara and Kathryn,' she
pressed on. 'I didn't know what any of you had done
to bring you here to Dad in the first place. I learnt a
lot about Ric's background. And Mitch's. But they
couldn't tell me anything about you, Johnny.'

'They had nothing to tell about me because there
is nothing,' he stated tersely. 'Both Ric and Mitch
have a family history. I don't.'

'But you must have a history,' Megan persisted,
determined to know. 'Even an orphan has a history.'

'None that I remember.' He shot her a glittery
look. 'I was told my mother was a prostitute who
died of a heroine overdose when I was two years old.
No-one claimed me and I was placed in foster care.
Whoever my biological father was—' he shook his
head '—no way of knowing.'

A two-year-old. Megan wondered how long it was

before someone had found him after his mother had overdosed. Probably best that he didn't remember.

'Your father was a father to me, Megan.'

Yes, she understood that. Yet... 'What of your foster parents, Johnny?'

Again he shook his head. 'There are people who should never be put in charge of children. I dropped out of the system when I was twelve. Went on the streets.'

Megan was shocked. He had spoken about abuse this morning, but how much abuse? What kind? She sensed he wasn't about to tell her. He was brushing over the bare facts as it was. She moved on to what he might answer.

'What about your education?'

'The best education I got was from your father. It has served me far better than any academic learning could.'

Her father again. She hadn't realised how very much he'd meant to a boy whose life had been empty of caring. Worse...a life that had surely been coloured by total mistrust of anyone—a smile to ward off evils.

'Where did you learn music?' she asked.

'The technical stuff from musicians. Guys in bands. But I made music in my head from very early on. It blocked out other things.'

And she had mocked his music as clever commercialism!

From what he'd said, even his songs were linked to what her father had taught him. Probably everything Johnny was now could be linked back to her father.

'Dad gave you a guitar,' she remembered.

'Yes, he did. I still have it. It's the one I play for our Christmas carols.'

What he'd been given here meant so much to him. So much. And her father had known it.

Why choose Johnny Ellis?

Because Johnny had been more *his adopted son* than the others?

Was she more his daughter than Jessie and Emily?

She liked to think so, yet she had no doubt he'd loved them all, each for her own different and very individual qualities. She hadn't ever really appreciated how lucky she and her sisters had been—brought up in an environment where caring for them was taken for granted, parents who loved them, listened to them, did their best to provide whatever was needed so they could pursue their interests.

Her childhood had been very happy. Her teens had been mostly a fun time, though she'd missed Gundamurra while she was at boarding school. It was only her fixation on Johnny that had blighted her later years.

Not his fault.

She'd acted like a spoiled bitch because he hadn't come to her party, hadn't fulfilled the role she'd cast for him. So she'd cast him in another role that didn't fit him, either.

Well, her perception of him had certainly been changed today. The problem was…it made him even more attractive to her.

'I haven't said I'm sorry…for *your* loss.' She squeezed his hand to impress her sincerity on him. 'I am, Johnny.'

His gaze swung back to her and it seemed to hold the dark intensity of eternal night—no stars. 'Will you stand with me tomorrow? At the graveside? Patrick put us together, Megan. I want us to be together.'

Her own desire for togetherness with him—far beyond what he was asking—zinged through her entire body, twisting her insides, heating her blood. She hoped he couldn't see the rush of heat to her face. 'Yes,' she whispered, her throat almost too tight to speak.

'Thank you.'

For a moment the air seemed charged with a sense of closeness that wildly fired up all Megan's hopes and dreams. Johnny rose to his feet, pulling her up with him. Her heart started galloping. He dropped her hand and she thought he meant to draw her into an embrace. The yearning for it inside her swamped any cautious thought she might have had.

She heard his sharply indrawn breath, saw his broad chest lift, expand, and looked up to find his head bent towards hers. His hands clamped around her upper arms. His gaze fastened on her mouth. Her own pent-up breath parted her lips. Anticipation kicked through her mind, scattering all her wits. He was going to kiss her. Johnny Ellis was going to kiss her.

But he spoke instead.

'I always used to think of you as my little sister, Megan.'

No-o-o-o... The silent scream reverberated around her head.

'If you could think of me…as your big brother…standing by you…'

No…no…no!

'…I think your father would like that.'

Rebellion cried this had nothing to do with her father. Nothing!

'You should go to bed and try to rest now,' he said, his smile a twist of brotherly caring. And he dropped a kiss on *her forehead*. 'Goodnight, Megan.'

He released her arms, backed off, turned, and headed across the lawn to the guest wing which housed his room.

She clenched her hands, the urge to fight, to hurl herself after him and beat out every shred of brotherly feeling, was barely containable. Pride forced her to hold still. Common sense directed her to go to her own room, shut the door and wait until tomorrow.

Tomorrow she would show him she was a woman, not a little girl. Her femininity would not be *neutered* by men's clothes. As for her hair…

She would *show* him.

No way was she going to let him pigeonhole her as *his little sister!*

CHAPTER SIX

JOHNNY was totally stunned by Megan's appearance the next morning. Not only was she wearing a curve-hugging black suit with a flirty little frill at the bottom of her skirt—drawing attention to the feminine shapeliness of her calves, fine ankles, and feet shod in sexy black high heels—but her hair was... positively mesmerising.

All throughout breakfast he could not stop looking at it. Usually she wore it in pigtails or scaped into a knot, tightly confined, with a hat crammed over it more often than not. He could not remember ever seeing it like this—lustrous red-gold waves springing softly from her head, cascading into curls that bounced alluringly around her shoulders. It looked so vivid against the paleness of her skin, and formed an amazingly rich, sensual contrast to her sombre attire.

Her face seemed different, too. Maybe it was the startling beauty of her hair framing it, or the subtle touches of make-up—brows pencilled a shade darker, a smoky shadow applied to her eyelids, enhancing the shape and size of her eyes, lending a more feminine mystique to their sharp directness, and the red-brown lipstick certainly added an enticing lushness to her mouth. He had imagined she could look quite striking if she tried. He simply wasn't prepared for...stunning!

She wore a double strand of pearls around her throat. They looked like the pearls he'd chosen for her twenty-first birthday. A grown-up necklace he'd thought at the time, something really good to commemorate her coming of age, Patrick's youngest daughter. He'd bought them in Broome, Picard pearls, the best in the world. He'd meant to present them himself at Megan's birthday party, but Liesel— leaving her had been impossible just then.

Seven years since Megan had turned twenty-one.

He'd sent the pearls and forgotten about them.

There had been Liesel's death…and all the promise of her talent lost.

Now Patrick's death.

He should be thinking of the man, not his daughter.

Johnny tried to keep his mind focussed on paying his last respects to Patrick Maguire. Yet even at the funeral service his attention was split. Megan sat beside him and every time she bent her head he was distracted by the rippling flow of her hair, the scent of it reminding him of fresh lemons, slightly tart but light and refreshing, completely unlike the erotic muskiness of other women's perfume.

And she stood beside him as Patrick was buried in the designated plot beside his beloved wife. With the extra elevation of high heels, the top of her head came up to his chin. Not as little as he had thought her. She held herself with very straight and tall dignity. Patrick would have been proud of her.

Afterwards, when they returned to the homestead, Johnny could not stop his gaze from following her every move—greeting the guests who'd flown in to attend the wake, graciously listening to what they wanted to say, serving them with drinks or food. Many people *he* didn't know had come, but *she* knew them all and their connections to her father. It brought home to Johnny that this was her life and he had only ever been a visitor to Gundamurra, not an integral part of it.

The people who lived on the station knew him, welcomed his company, chatted to him. Somehow it wasn't enough. He wanted to be at Megan's side, sharing the responsibilities of outback hospitality, familiar with everything that was familiar to her. The sense of being an outsider—*the pop-star*—grated on him, especially when Megan's attention was courted by young men attached to other pastoral properties.

Men who were smitten by the way she looked today.

Men who won kind smiles from her.

Men who might be eager to offer themselves as partners, given some sign of encouragement.

Johnny's charm started to wear thin.

A previously unknown possessive streak hit him, driving him to insert himself into the private little *tête-à-têtes* these men sought with Megan, making his presence at her side felt and forcibly acknowledged. Though that didn't work too well. He found himself viewed as a curiosity, not a threat to their interests.

He managed to hold himself back from crassly declaring that *he* now owned forty-nine percent of Gundamurra, which he'd saved from the brink of bankruptcy, so Patrick's daughter was not quite the attractive prospect they might imagine her to be.

Futile move anyway, he argued to himself. How she looked today was drawcard enough.

Perhaps he was less than subtle in cutting out one guy who was definitely coming on to her. Megan threw him a look of exasperation and grittily declared, 'I do not need a big brother standing over me, Johnny.'

He'd never felt less like a big brother.

'Seems like you're not sour on all men after all,' he shot back at her.

Her eyes widened.

Johnny realised he sounded jealous. He *was* jealous. He wished he'd given in to the temptation to kiss her last night, kiss her so hard she wouldn't be thinking of giving any other guy the time of day. He wanted to grab her arm and haul her away from everyone else right now, have her to himself, convince her that he was the man for her.

But was he?

And what damage might he do to the working partnership they had to have, if he made the move and it was wrong for her?

'I'm just trying to be as good a hostess as my mother,' she said, her chin lifting in defiance of his criticism.

'Right! Well, I'll leave you to it.'

He backed off, sternly reminding himself of the company they were in—people here for Patrick. However, he spent the rest of the wake simmering with frustration, though he took considerable satisfaction in the number of glances Megan threw his way. She'd well and truly disturbed him. Let her be disturbed, too!

He was glad when all the guests were gone and he could busy himself helping with the cleaning up, chatting with Evelyn in the kitchen, feeling *at home* again. There was no formal dinner tonight. The family picked at leftovers, flaking out in the sitting room once the homestead was back to normal. The consensus of opinion was that the wake had been all it should have been for a man of Patrick Maguire's standing—a man who would be sadly missed by many.

Emotional and physical fatigue gradually took its toll, people trailing off to bed until there was only Johnny and Megan left in the room. He was sprawled in an armchair. She was on a sofa, one elbow propped on its armroll, legs up, her stockinged feet bare of the shoes she had kicked off. It was a pose that seductively outlined the very female curve of waist, hip and thigh, and Johnny found it difficult not to let his gaze linger on it.

He expected her to leave. She usually did avoid being alone with him. Any moment now those legs would swing off the sofa, take her away to the privacy of her room, and it was probably better that they did, save him from making a fool of himself. He watched her feet, waiting for them to move. She wriggled her toes. His gaze dropped to the shoes lying beside the sofa, noting the long, narrow shape of them.

'Cramped feet?' he asked.

'They're not used to wearing fashionable shoes,' she drily admitted.

'Want me to massage them?'

'Is that a big brotherly thing to do?'

The mocking taunt whipped his gaze up to meet the smoking challenge she was directing straight at him.

Megan could no longer contain the furious frustration that had been welling up in her all day. 'I am not your little sister and I do not need you to watch over me,' she threw at him in seething protest over how he had acted with her—last night, holding her hand and kissing her forehead as though she were a baby, keeping close to her today, ready to be supportive at any falter on her part, inserting himself at her side whenever he thought she might not be able to handle what he interpreted as possibly unwelcome attention.

He hitched himself forward in his chair, gesturing for understanding, frowning over her reaction. 'It was just a friendly offer, Megan.'

Friendly!

For him to now sit on the other end of the sofa and nursemaid her to the extent of massaging her toes... It would drive her so crazy she'd probably end up needling his crotch with them! She swung her legs off the sofa and stood up, viewing him with bristling *hauteur*.

'I'm fine. What's more, I'm all grown up, Johnny, in case you haven't noticed. Which you should have, since I made the effort not to *neuter* myself today.'

He grimaced. 'Impossible not to notice.'

'So what did I get wrong?'

'Wrong?'

'You weren't moved to make any positive comment.' She lifted her arms and tossed her hair back over her shoulders in angry impatience with it hanging around her face—hair she'd spent over an hour shampooing and blow-drying so it would look fluffy and feminine. 'Still not good enough for you!' she muttered, mocking herself more than him.

'Not good enough?' he repeated incredulously, shaking his head as though hopelessly confused by her attitude.

Of course her words made no sense in the context of his *little sister* mind frame. Totally incensed by his insensitivity to this major attempt at changing his view of her, Megan clenched her jaw and headed for the liquor cabinet at the other end of the room, determined on blotting out the stupid futility of trying to change anything where Johnny was concerned.

'Well, I'm certainly old enough to get drunk tonight,' she tossed at him derisively. 'Entitled to, what's more. So why don't you go off to bed, Johnny, and leave me to drown my sorrows?'

He suddenly exploded off his chair, grabbing her arm as she moved past him. 'What do you mean by...*not good enough?*' He bit out the words as though they were killing him. His eyes slashed at hers, trying to cut through to her soul.

The intensity coming from him pumped Megan up to defy him further. 'You didn't even notice I was wearing the pearls you gave me for my twenty-first birthday,' she rattled out recklessly. 'On the other hand, why should you? You probably got some aide to buy a suitable gift and send it to me.'

'I did notice them,' he fiercely refuted her. 'I chose them myself. And I was pleased to see you wearing them.'

'You didn't *say* anything!'

'What do you want me to say? That you look fantastic? That I could hardly keep my eyes off you? That I wanted to beat every other man away?'

A sense of wild triumph zinged around Megan's brain. She had succeeded in getting to him as a man. Johnny Ellis had actually been *jealous* of the guys who'd shown her some admiration. He *had* seen her as a woman with the power to attract male interest.

It was a huge step forward, but where did it get her if he wasn't prepared to act on it? 'So you think I need your protection now?' she flung at him.

'It's the last thing on my mind.'

The emphatic beat of his voice was like thunder in her ears, thunder in her heart. And she got action aplenty. He stepped closer, scooping her body around to face him. The hand that had seized her arm lifted, its fingers raking through her hair, dragging her head back so that it was tilted up to his. The raw desire flaring from his eyes made her stomach quiver in anticipation.

Johnny Ellis wanted her.

His mouth crashed down onto hers in a passionate plundering that incited an equally passionate response, years of wanting pouring into her need to taste *this* man, have him tasting her, wanting more of her. She wound her arms around his neck, stretched up on tiptoe, pressed closer, trying to lock in every possible physical contact with him, revelling in the exciting heat of his big strong body, the tension in his muscles.

He kissed her as greedily and urgently as she kissed him. When he sucked in air, she did, too, her pulse racing, her breasts heaving to the same rise and fall of his chest. Though even the slightest pause in this hectic intimacy hit a panic button. She didn't want him to stop, to pull away from her, have second thoughts about what he was doing. She kept a tight hold on him, her fingers thrusting through his hair, curling around his head, rabidly encouraging continuance.

He kissed her some more, with a deepening eroticism that stirred her desire for him into a chaotic frenzy, every nerve in her body sizzling for the fulfilment of all he promised. His hands roved over her back, following its curves, curling over the taut mounds of her bottom, squeezing, lifting, fitting her more closely to him. No doubt about how strongly he was aroused. She felt his erection against her stomach and exulted in the blatant physical power of his desire for her.

Then he tore his mouth from hers and buried his face in her hair, rubbing his cheeks over it, breathing in the scent on it, tasting it with hot sensual kisses. And she pressed her own face into the warm hollow of his neck, savouring the smell of him, her sensitised lips picking up the rapid throb of his pulse beat there, enclosing it, sucking on it, excited by his excitement and wildly wanting to drive it higher and higher.

'Megan...'

The hoarse whisper carried the sound of raging need, making her heart leap with fierce exhilaration. His throat moved in a convulsive swallow.

'Megan...' A stronger tone, harsh with urgency. 'Tell me—' intense command '—is this right for you?'

'Yes...yes,' she answered, every fibre of her being affirming its rightness for her.

'You know I have to leave tomorrow,' he said in strained argument.

'I don't care,' she cried recklessly.

'Then neither do I,' he muttered savagely, and Megan found herself abruptly swept off her feet, her legs hanging over his arm, the rest of her clamped to his chest, and he was carrying her out of the sitting room. 'Better than drowning your sorrows in a bottle,' he bit out, apparently still needing to convince himself he wasn't doing wrong by her.

'Yes,' she agreed emphatically. 'Much better.'

'Your room or mine?'

'Mine.' Where she had dreamed so many times of Johnny Ellis coming to love her. Years of dreams. Never any substance to them. At least she was about to experience some physical reality of all those secret desires, even if it was only sex.

When he stepped out on the verandah, he hesitated. 'I don't have any protection with me.'

'I told you I don't need your protection.'

'Right!'

Relieved of any worries about getting her pregnant, he surged forward again, striding out, legs pumping with driven purpose as he headed straight for her room. Megan had no protection at all against the possibility of conception, but she didn't care. She hung on to him, recklessly abandoning every care.

It didn't matter what was said.

Didn't matter what was done.

As long as she had Johnny Ellis in her bed tonight!

CHAPTER SEVEN

JOHNNY'S mind was in total ferment, but his body kept moving, driven by its own physical need to satisfy the desire roaring through him. As he'd stepped out on the verandah, the cooler air of the outback night had hit him in the face, sobering him enough to realise what he was doing…taking Patrick's daughter to bed with him. Yet Megan wanted it, too. She was clinging to him. No second thoughts from her.

And she *was* grown up. Well and truly grown up. Even prepared for sex, having her own form of protection since she didn't need him to use anything. Which meant he'd been completely wrong about her attitude to *all men*. She couldn't have been sour on them. Only him. So why was she letting him do this? More than that, actively stirring him into it.

Pride stung by the comments he'd made about her yesterday?

Using sex to take away the bitter taste of her father's death?

Using *him* because he was here and she thought he was the kind of man who would view it as meaningless?

He reached her door, opened it. His heart was rocketing around his chest as he carried her inside. The ache in his groin demanded that he stop thinking and simply take what was being offered. He closed the door, switched on the light, his mind fiercely dictating that Megan not hide him in darkness.

He set her on her feet, cupped her face in his hands, forcing her gaze to meet his. 'It's *me…* Johnny,' he said, searching her eyes with gut-wrenching intensity for answers he could live with. 'Sure you want this, Megan?'

Angry defiance sparked. 'Getting cold feet, Johnny? Want to put me back into the *little sister* box?'

'No, I don't!' exploded from him.

The sparkles changed to glittery challenge. 'Then don't treat me like an idiot child. We're here. And yes, I'm sure.'

He stopped caring about what was in her mind. The desire burning inside him flared up, took control, directing the paths it wanted to take. His hands slid slowly down the long elegant neck that held her head so high. Her skin was warm, soft, silky smooth. She stood absolutely still, watching him, absorbing his touch without the slightest flinch. The sensual trail of his fingers was interrupted by the necklace at the base of her throat.

His pearls.

Leave them there.

He wanted her stripped of everything else but not them. The pearls were a link to him. They had meaning. He lifted them, rubbed them between his fingers, knowing their lustre was increased by contact with flesh—her flesh—his.

'Why did you wear them today?' he asked, wanting it to be significant.

Still the challenge sizzling at him. 'Why not? You

gave them to me to wear. They looked good with my black suit.'

Denying them any personal meaning yet all his instincts insisted it was there—if only as a weapon in her armoury to get at him. Flaunting her hair, her figure, *his* necklace…was it just some sexual battle she was waging?

The primitive survivor in Johnny stirred.

Regardless of what was driving Megan, he would win out in the end.

And get it right.

Megan sucked in a quick nervous breath as the skin-tingling pads of his fingers glided down the edges of her jacket's V neckline. Panic was still blurring her mind. She'd thought he was going to stop, back off. The white-hot need for intimacy was no longer out-running control and she couldn't bring herself to force it by throwing herself at him. They were here in her bedroom. He had to want her…want her so much nothing would stop him.

She shouldn't have hit out with that negative stuff, reminding him of the years between them, pretending that his necklace was just a necklace.

But he wasn't backing off.

It *was* happening.

And she was scared stiff that he'd find her hope-lessly inadequate at meeting him as an equal when they were finally in bed together, that he'd realise how relatively inexperienced she was and wish he hadn't been tempted into having any sexual connec-tion with her.

She'd only been thinking of satisfying herself before.

But that wasn't enough.

She wanted Johnny to love her, need her, come back to her.

With tantalising slowness he undid the top button of her jacket. Then the next. And the next. Her breasts seemed to swell with a terribly tight feeling. Yet her legs were turning into wobbly jelly. He slid her jacket off her shoulders, caressed her arms as he pushed the sleeves down. Her skin broke out in goose bumps. She had to *do* something or she'd end up paralysed by inhibitions.

His coat and tie had been discarded after the visitors had left, the sleeves of his shirt rolled up when he'd been helping in the kitchen. As his hands moved around her back to undo her bra, the thought of being stripped naked while he was still dressed galvanised Megan into action. She attacked the buttons on his shirt, needing to rip it off him as fast as she could, keep some kind of equality between them.

Once he'd dispensed with her bra, he helped, tossing his shirt on the floor to join the other discarded clothes, then removing her skirt while she hesitated over touching his trousers. She'd seen Johnny naked to the waist before—washing up outside many times. The beautifully sculpted masculinity of his chest and arms held no surprises for her, but close up like this, with the taut muscles and smooth hairless skin barely a heartbeat away from the tips of her bare breasts, she was too caught up in breathless anticipation to even attempt stripping him further.

Besides, he did it fast enough, revealing himself

without any worry whatsoever about her reaction to *his* completely naked body. No doubt he was perfectly comfortable in his own skin. And why wouldn't he be? On any male scale he was magnificently built. Impossible for him to feel any sense of inadequacy with so much blatant power in his physique.

Her stillness, her staring, evoked a gruff taunt from him. 'Not freezing up on me, are you, Megan?'

Her chin jerked up, eyes flaring a bold challenge. 'Just looking.' This was no time for backing down!

'Satisfied?'

'I hope I will be.'

Something like an animal growl issued from his throat. His hands spanned her waist. She was lifted off her feet, carried swiftly to the bed, laid down so he could stand back and look at her. Which he did, taking in every detail of her from the spill of her hair on the pillow to the uncontrollable curling of her toes. Megan wanted to close her eyes but she couldn't allow herself that weakness. It would betray the nervous fear pumping through her. She watched him, waiting for his response, her heart drumming in her ears.

Johnny could barely contain himself. She lay there in seductive abandonment, her hair a fiery halo, her arms lying loosely across the bed, waiting to wrap around him when he came to her, the lushly full breasts peaking their invitation, her pale skin gleaming like sensual satin. He'd lose himself in her in no time flat if he wasn't careful.

No way was he going to leave Megan thinking of

him as a rutting animal. If she wanted that kind of perverse satisfaction, she wasn't about to get it. Nor would he let her dismiss him as just another man. God only knew how many lovers she'd had but he was all fired up to be the one who lingered longest in her memory, the one she'd want more than any other.

She was still wearing the sheer black pantihose that had drawn his attention to the shapeliness of her legs. He leaned one knee on the bed, hooked his thumbs under the waistband and rolled the garment down, slowly easing it over her hips.

She lifted herself slightly to allow it free passage past the sexy cheeks of her bottom. He smiled at the natural triangle of red-gold pubic hair, glad it hadn't been subjected to a bikini or Brazilian wax. The fiery arrow, pointing to the apex of her silky thighs, was much more exciting.

He caressed the erotic curves of her legs as he removed the black nylon, her feet, her toes, and there was certainly nothing *brotherly* about what he did. The slight twitches and gasps from Megan told him the prolonged sensuality was getting to her. He wanted to weave such an enthralling web of it she'd be totally captivated, aware of only him and how he was touching her, making love to her.

He trailed kisses up and down her inner thighs, revelling in the revealing quiver of her flesh under his lips as he moved her legs apart. He caressed the soft folds of her sex, feeling the moist heat that telegraphed her readiness for him. Not yet, he told himself, fighting the urge to take, to sate his own almost bursting need for her.

He grazed his mouth over the erotic little hollows under her hipbones while inciting her need to a higher pitch with his hand, his thumb gently rubbing her clitoris, fingers circling, diving inside her, working a teasing rhythm as he pressed hot kisses over her stomach. And her body arched up to him, inviting, inciting.

But he wanted her wild for him.

He ran his tongue around the tips of her breasts and she broke into chaotic movement, hands clawing at his back, urging an upward surge. Excitement flooded through him but he denied her demand to hurry the pace, surrounding the taut thrust of her nipple with his mouth, drawing on it, reinforcing the rhythmic caress he'd maintained, building an arc of throbbing pleasure.

She grabbed his head, fingers tugging his hair. He moved to her other breast, determined on having her whole body acutely aware of him, craving and wallowing in every nuance of sensation he could give her. Her body thrashed from side to side in a chaotic offering that drove him to almost frenzied action. Impossible to hold out much longer.

He drew himself up, hovered over her, his eyes seeking affirmation of all he felt in hers. Shards of silver were fiercely shot at him. Her legs curled around his thighs, convulsively pressing. Her hands linked around his neck, trying to pull him down to her. She was panting with the primitive passion he had stirred.

Whether it was pride or possessiveness or some dark streak of male domination driving him, Johnny didn't know, but the powerful need to stamp himself in her mind overrode everything else.

'Say my name,' he commanded, resisting the compelling pressure to perform at her instigation. 'Say it!'

'Johnny...' It burst from her as though her mind was filled to overflowing with it.

His heart leapt in exultation. He positioned himself to enter her, pausing to feel the pulsing welcome of her inner muscles closing around him, sucking him in.

'Again,' he insisted.

'Johnny...' It was an anguished plea.

He picked up her fluttering hands and slammed them above her head as he drove himself deeply into the sweet hot cavern of her innermost self. He lay on the soft cushion of her breasts, his face directly above hers. He wanted eye contact but her lids were shut, her mouth open, dragging in quick shallow breaths.

'Look at me!' he commanded.

The lashes flew up. Her eyes seemed unfocussed, inwardly concentrated, but they swam back to seeing him squarely.

'Know me as you feel me, Megan,' he said more softly, and kissed her, wanting to engage her in a sense of total intimacy with him, with the Johnny Ellis she had scorned for so long but was now accepting with all her being.

Megan was swamped with tidal wave after tidal wave of incredible sensation. The unrelenting swell of it had crashed through any inhibitions she might have had long before Johnny had finally plunged into this ultimate joining with her. Now she simply rode with it, incapable of doing anything else, marvelling at the exquisite peaks of pleasure, the ripple effect through her entire body, the almost torturous tension of anticipating more and more, the ecstatic feeling of letting herself go, melting around him.

In the hazy recesses of a mind drowning in intense feeling, there lurked the exhilarating satisfaction that this was, indeed, Johnny Ellis making love to her. And if she'd been waiting her whole life for this, it was worth the waiting. She didn't question why he'd demanded she say his name. Her thought processes were far too adrift for questioning anything. She'd wanted to say it, anyway, wanted to taste it, savour it, shout it, identifying and claiming him as the only man who had ever moved her this deeply.

As for knowing him...it was knowledge she had craved, knowledge she was now exulting in, knowledge she would hug to herself forever. It was awesome, fantastic, the glorious sense of rolling from one climax to another, pinnacles of creamy pleasure, then finally the faster pumping of his need, spilling into wild spasms of release, Johnny letting go, surrendering control to her as his powerful body shuddered into relaxation, accepting her readily loving embrace.

Conscious of his weight on her, he rolled onto his side, but he didn't disentangle himself from her. She stroked him, adoring his strength, wanting to touch as she hadn't dared touch before. It dawned on her how passive she had been while he did...everything!

Absorbing the feelings he'd aroused had stunned

her into a weird submission, as though she was in a time and place where only what he was doing to her had any reality—an immediate and overwhelming reality that compelled intense concentration.

Only now did she realise she hadn't made any effort to pleasure him. Hadn't even thought of it. Was he satisfied with how it had been? Would he want more of her when he hadn't been given any active demonstration of desire *from* her?

She hadn't exactly been a log, but…

'Content?' he asked.

It sounded as though he'd been working hard to give her satisfaction and wanted to be assured of it.

'Are you?' she tossed back, worried about not matching up to his previous sexual partners.

He shifted, propping himself up on his elbow, smoothing her hair away from her face with his other hand, eyeing her with brooding frustration. 'What is it with you, Megan? You can't concede a straight answer?'

Aware that she was being defensive again, she tried a rueful smile. 'Sorry, Johnny. You're a fantastic lover. Thank you for being so…so giving.'

He returned her smile. 'Then you do feel content?'

'How could I not? You've completely rocked me with a truly brilliant experience,' she said flippantly, wary of placing too much weight on what could very well be a one-night stand.

Rocked her… Was that another hit at his career? Johnny's sense of satisfaction that he had reached Megan deep down was instantly shaken by insecurities.

Maybe she had just been using him…Johnny on the spot.

And he had performed his heart out for her.

Brilliant…

'Well, I'm glad I'm good for something…apart from money,' he mocked.

He saw her eyes blank with shock, then spark with alarm. Her hand lifted swiftly to his face, cupping his cheek, instinctively needing to reach into him as she rushed into earnest speech.

'I'm sorry if that came out wrong, Johnny. It's just that…you're going tomorrow…and I have to let you go…so…'

'Easier to put me back in the box you've had me in for years, Megan?'

She grimaced. 'That is where you live most of your life. No point in my wanting it otherwise.'

He asked the crucial question. 'Do you want it otherwise?'

Her lashes dropped. She watched the trail of her hand as it slid down his throat and over the bunched muscles of his shoulder. She drew a deep breath and wryly said, 'Let's be realistic, Johnny. You're here tonight, gone tomorrow, and I don't know if you'll ever be back.'

'I'll be back,' he stated unequivocally. 'As soon as the movie is wrapped up.'

'Mmm…'

To his ears it was the hum of disbelief. Why wasn't she prepared to accept his word for it? He'd never lied to her, never given false promises. Still, there was no way to prove he would return until he did.

She was gently rotating her palm over his nipple, seemingly fascinated by the fact that it could respond like hers to caressing. It surprised him when she leaned over to take it in her mouth and her hand glided down, over his stomach, touching him, stroking him. Excitement instantly buzzed. This was hard evidence that she still wanted him, no matter what the future held.

He rolled onto his back, carrying her with him, letting her do whatever she wanted with his body, letting the pleasure of it stream through him. He played with her beautiful hair, running his fingers through its silkiness, winding it around them, wishing he could bind her to him just as easily. But the reality was…only time could do that. So he wanted to make the most of now.

He was fully aroused again, teetering on the brink of climax. He quickly lifted her to sit astride him, wanting her to do the taking, wanting to watch her loving him, if only physically. The necklace of pearls swung back and forth as she settled into a rhythm— a metronome measuring the escalation of excitement. He cupped her breasts, wanting to feel the beat of her flesh on his everywhere…soft, hot music to his soul.

She paused, her eyes glittering with stormy feeling. 'Say *my* name, Johnny.'

He smiled at the echo of his primal need to be known by her. 'Megan…'

'Again!' she fiercely insisted.

'Megan Maguire,' he rolled out like the rich chord of a song that gripped his heart—a song he was yet to write but it was beating through his mind.

'Yes.' It was a hiss of satisfaction. 'I am my father's daughter and don't you ever forget it, Johnny Ellis,' she added proudly, tossing her hair back over her shoulders as though it was a mane.

Then she rode him hard, and Johnny was racing with her, exhilarated by the frenetic energy behind making him come, loving the sight of her driving them both to an intense climax, the pearls whipping around her throat. His pearls…his woman…Patrick's daughter…

It felt so good to hold her afterwards. No tension. No sense of conflict running between them. It was as though she gave herself to him without reservation, her body folding into the curve of his, spoon-fashion, happy with being close, relaxing into languorous contentment. No question about that now. There was a sense of peace in the silence, though Johnny knew there were other questions that would have to be answered in the future.

Had Patrick foreseen this connection between him and Megan?

Had he made his will with a marriage in mind?

Home is where the heart is, Johnny thought, but Megan didn't believe his heart was in the life at Gundamurra. He had to show her it was so.

She heaved a deep sigh, then quietly asked, 'If you chose these pearls for me personally, Johnny, why didn't you come to my party and give them to me?'

He raised his head from the pillow, looked over her shoulder. She was fingering the necklace as though wondering if it really did mean anything.

He kissed her shoulder. 'I planned to, Megan. I'd booked my flight home. Then I learnt a close friend of mine had been taken to hospital, overdosed on heroin. I hoped I could talk her into wanting to live.'

'Her?'

'I don't know if the name would mean anything to you...Liesel Furner?'

'No. It doesn't ring any bells.'

'Liesel had some brief fame as a torch singer. Her voice was very powerful, very emotional, very passionate. A great talent...but also a deeply screwed-up person. She...gave up on herself...and I couldn't pull her out of the darkness.'

'You cared about her.'

He paused before answering, looking back, remembering how he'd felt. Impossible to explain an experience to someone who had never been driven into those dark prisons of the mind by the abuse of others. Mitch and Ric would have understood, but Megan? He didn't want her to take her there. Not tonight.

He used a simple parallel. 'I would have liked someone to care about my mother, Megan.'

Another deep sigh. 'I'm sorry, Johnny. I guess you're saying Liesel died, too.'

'It didn't matter what I said...what I did...she didn't have the will to survive.'

'But she must have known you cared. At least she had that.'

While Megan had thought he didn't care about her.

No difficulty in reading that equation.

And the truth was...Liesel's life had meant more to him than anybody's birthday party. The childhood abuse she'd suffered had struck a strong empathy in him. He'd wanted to give her what Patrick had given him, get her head around all the negatives, lead her into…

But he'd failed.

And it had taken him a while to get past that failure.

When he'd come home again, Megan had gone off to agricultural college. And ever after that, she'd removed herself from him, actively driving him away from any sense of closeness with her.

'I'm sorry I disappointed you. It wasn't that I didn't care…'

'You were dealing with your own life,' she finished for him, a wry touch of resignation in her voice. 'And that's how it is, Johnny—you dealing with your life, me dealing with mine.'

We've shared tonight, he wanted to argue, but he knew one night wouldn't carry much weight with her.

It was a beginning, he told himself, and settled back down to hold her as long as he could.

CHAPTER EIGHT

STRANGE how calm she felt the next morning after Johnny had left her to go to his own room, mindful of the untimely aspect of their intimacy if it were known. It had been a very private interlude, just between them, and they'd agreed it should stay private. Especially since he was leaving today.

Megan wryly wondered if she had finally grown up, accepting what couldn't be changed, respecting what should be respected. The rebellious turmoil incited by her father's will was gone. The bitter scorn she'd nurtured towards Johnny and his career had been ill-founded, fed by her own self-absorbed needs and totally unfair. It, too, was gone. In its place was a far more sympathetic appreciation of the person Johnny was and what drove him.

She still wanted him. More than ever after last night. But she knew she had to let him go, release him from any sense of responsibility towards her. What had happened between them had been more her doing than his. She'd made the decisions, pushing him into giving her a very real taste of the man he was.

A generous lover…a generous person in every sense…and it was time for her to be generous to him. No snipes. No clinging. Just let him go to be whatever he wanted—needed—to be.

She put the pearl necklace back in its jewellery

box, then washed and dressed in her usual shirt and jeans, conscious of feeling no need to be aggressive or provocative about anything today. The sense of putting away her life to this point before embarking on the next phase was very strong.

Her father would not be with her anymore. Johnny was going this morning. Mitch, Ric, their wives, her sisters and their husbands…they were all flying out, as well. She would be left to get on with the task of managing Gundamurra as best she could, with the financial backing Johnny had set up and put at her disposal. This was what all her life had been building towards…following in her father's footsteps. It was time to take it on now and make a success of it.

Everyone came to the dining room for breakfast, probably conscious of its being their last meal in each other's company for a while. Possibly a long while. Megan wondered if Mitch and Ric would ever return to Gundamurra, now that her father was gone, though both of them were very solicitous towards her.

'If any problem arises that I can deal with, call me,' Mitch urged earnestly. 'No hesitation, Megan. Just call me. Okay? Any legal thing you want explained, or you're worried about, or something you want cleared with Johnny…'

The message was loud and clear. He was there for her. As her father had been for him.

It was the same with Ric, though his concern was more personal, taking the chair beside her at the table to speak privately. 'Megan, if Johnny starts treading on your toes, taking over what he should leave to you, let me know and I'll talk to him. I have no doubt he'd mean well, but Patrick made you the boss here and that's how it should be. So any time you need a mediator, I know Johnny will listen to me. Just lay it out and I'll handle it. Okay?'

All three of them, determined on giving support—her father's *boys*. And although there was no blood relationship between them, they truly were a band of brothers, Megan thought, probably closer than real family in their knowledge and understanding of each other.

They were her father's legacy, too, she realised, not just Gundamurra. Stepping in as brothers to her, as well, except she'd never wanted Johnny as a brother. Had her father known that? Had he written his will with the deliberate intent of forcing both of them to deal with each other, hoping for an outcome that would at least sort out her feelings, one way or another?

He'd known far more of Johnny than she had.

Maybe he'd simply aimed for her to learn who Johnny was—the real person behind the image. A major lesson about making judgements, not letting emotions rule, standing back and using informed reason, putting herself in another's shoes, treading gently instead of blindly stomping. *Being worthy of her father*...Mitch's words...finally struck home to her.

Johnny had seated himself directly across the table and she was acutely aware of him watching her over breakfast—concern in his eyes, too. 'I'd like a private chat with you before I go, Megan,' he pressed.

'Sure, Johnny.' Her smile was to show everyone they were *friends* now, no acrimony souring the partnership they had to have. 'Let's walk down to the airstrip together. Mitch can take the Land Rover to carry the luggage and everyone else. I'll see you all fly off in the plane, then drive back to the homestead.'

There was a hard moment, filled with the nervous tension of wanting him to understand it was better to skip past the physical intimacy they'd shared, just leave it behind them. Meeting in a room would make that difficult for her. His attraction was too strong, the sexual memories too fresh.

His eyes searched hers with a sharp intensity that suggested he wanted to fight this arrangement, seek a more exclusive time of closure with her. It was a huge relief when he nodded, conceding to what would be a far less fraught situation for her, being out in the open with the evidence of the drought all around them, a pertinent reminder of what their partnership was essentially about—rescuing Gundamurra.

Thankfully Evelyn provided some distraction, coming in to fuss over him, as usual, ensuring he was served with the crispy bacon he liked. For once, Megan could smile at the housekeeper's desire to indulge his preferences. How many people did care about Johnny Ellis at such a basic level, expecting nothing back except the pleasure of giving him pleasure? He'd never had loving parents. It was good that Evelyn added to his sense of being home here at Gundamurra.

Megan wanted him to come back.

He'd said he would.

She hoped her blatantly *wanton* behaviour last

night would not cause him to reconsider. If he thought she expected a continuing affair with him...

The bottom-line truth was she did want it.

But did he?

Somehow she had to make him feel free to choose. Her heart cringed at the thought of him nursing any sense of obligation towards her, especially in a sexual sense.

This was very much on her mind when the time of departure came. Jessie and Emily weren't leaving until after lunch, so they and their husbands had joined her on the front verandah to say their farewells to the others. Everyone hugged and kissed. The Land Rover set off for the airstrip where Johnny's Cessna was waiting for them, ready to fly them back to Sydney. Megan waited for the dust to settle in the vehicle's wake before setting off with Johnny, who seemed perfectly relaxed, amiably chatting to her sisters.

Charm, she thought, wishing she knew what it was papering over today.

'Time to go,' he finally said, shook hands with the men, kissed her sisters' cheeks, then caught Megan's hand to lead her down the steps.

He kept possession of it, his strong fingers tightly enveloping hers as they began their walk together. Megan made no attempt to extract them from his hold. She didn't even care if it was a big-brotherly link. It was good to feel his touch again, good that he wanted to touch her.

What she had to project now was dignity and grace. Never mind that her insides were churning with the need to hang on to this man. He was under contract to finish his movie. Begging him to stay was not an option, anyway.

'Megan…you *will* use the money,' he said forcefully, his tone strained with uncertainty.

Why would he doubt it? Because of having sex with her last night? Did he think that might have somehow tainted his investment? That her pride would stop her from using it?

'Yes, I will, Johnny,' she assured him. 'Gundamurra needs it,' she added to put everything in its proper perspective.

'Right!' he agreed, relief obvious.

He cared about Gundamurra. That, at least, they had in common. But would he come back? They had walked past most of the buildings before Megan screwed up the necessary courage to say, 'I don't want you to feel bad about last night, Johnny. It's nothing for you to worry about.'

'Nothing?' He repeated the word as though it was intensely offensive.

Megan inwardly cringed. The last thing she wanted was to sound scornful of what he'd given her. Her mind whirled, seeking ways to fix his impression. 'I just meant…it was good for me.'

'But this is the cut-off line,' he muttered derisively.

She tried again. 'You're leaving. I don't want you to be concerned about it. That's all.'

'Over and done with.'

'I hope it was good for you, too,' she rushed out, hating the way he was bringing down the curtain when she desperately wanted him to keep caring about her.

His fingers almost crushed hers before he realised what he was doing and relaxed his grip. 'Will you e-mail me? Give me reports on how things are going here? I want to know, Megan,' he said tersely.

If it was a test for how she really felt about continuing a relationship with him, Megan was only too happy to comply with what he required. 'Yes, I will,' she said firmly.

'Good!' Again he squeezed her hand, but not as tightly as before.

Her head was almost giddy with relief. He was inviting her to have regular contact with him...if he replied to her e-mails. She couldn't really count on that. Once he was back to making his movie, caught up in such a different world over there...but he couldn't completely forget her. Even if he got involved with another woman, making love to her would trigger memories...wouldn't it?

Her stomach felt like a worm farm.

She fiercely told herself she had no personal claim on him. Had no right to make one. Yet everything within her burned with a deeply primitive desire to have him as hers and hers alone.

The Land Rover stood just ahead of them, Johnny's Cessna behind it, ready for take off.

'If the shooting of the movie runs to schedule, it should be finished in three months,' he informed her. 'Do you have any problem with my coming back then, Megan?'

'No,' she shot out, elated that *he* had no problem with it. 'You'll always be welcome home, Johnny,' she added as warmly as she could, acutely aware of not having welcomed him for far too many years.

He stopped, pausing her, as well. Drawn by the mountain of tension emanating from him, Megan half-turned, steeling herself to glance up at him. He stepped to face her full on, his free hand lifting, tilting back the wide-brimmed Akubra hat she always wore outside to protect her fair skin from the sun. His eyes were a piercing green, scouring hers for truth.

'Do you mean that, Megan?'

She held his gaze with determined steadiness. 'I do, Johnny. I'm deeply sorry I was such a mean bitch to you.' She managed an appealing little smile as she finally acknowledged, 'My father knew best.'

His face relaxed, returning a smile that held whimsical irony. 'Patrick…yes…I think he did.' His voice was furred with feelings, instantly stirring up her own.

A huge lump of emotion welled into her throat. Tears pricked her eyes. Desperate to keep this leave-taking on some kind of even keel, she babbled, 'I hope your movie goes well.'

Still the whimsical half smile. 'More important is the movie of my life.'

She didn't understand.

He saw the confusion in her eyes and quoted…

'"All the world's a stage,
   And all the men and women merely players:
   They have their exits and their entrances:
   And one man in his time plays many parts."
   Shakespeare.'

He gave the credit drily, then added, 'I'm not entirely uneducated, Megan.'

'You've taken out honours in the school of life, Johnny,' she quickly replied, wanting to acknowledge how wrong she'd been in her judgement of him.

He shook his head, as though his successes were irrelevant. 'I wish I didn't have to make this exit, leaving you with so much work to carry through alone.' His voice gathered an urgent intensity and he took both her hands in his in pressing persuasion. 'Promise me you'll let me know if you run into difficulties that seem insurmountable.'

And he'd come running to the rescue?

Maybe he would...for Gundamurra.

But for her?

'Okay. But this is my stage, Johnny,' she felt compelled to remind him. 'I know how to play it. And I don't want other roles. This is who I am.'

He nodded. His eyelids lowered to half-mast, thick lashes veiling the expression in his eyes. He took a deep breath as though inwardly gathering strength for what he had to say next. All Megan's senses were on sharp alert, anxious to glean some hint of what he was thinking. Yet when he spoke, they were simple words of farewell.

'Until next time.'

He leaned down and kissed her cheek, then stood back, smiling a full blast of Johnny Ellis charm.

'I like your hair loose. They say a woman's hair is her crowning glory. Yours outshines all the rest, Megan.'

His hands slid from hers and he was off, striding for the open door of the waiting plane.

Was her cheek better than her forehead? Megan wondered as she watched him go. Her hat would have made her forehead a harder place to reach. Better that he hadn't kissed her mouth, she told herself. It would have been too tempting to cling to him, turn it into more than a friendly goodbye kiss.

Next time, she kept repeating in her mind.

The door of the plane was closed.

She waited for Johnny to make this exit from her life, listening to the plane's engines starting up, watching the wheels begin to roll, picking up speed, lifting off the dirt airstrip, her eyes following the flight of the Cessna until it was a distant speck in the sky.

Only then did she realise she'd been winding her hair around her fingers—hair she'd left loose this morning because she hadn't wanted to look *neutered.*

It outshines all the rest, he'd said.

She wanted to believe it wasn't just charm, that his last smile to her meant that he did see her as a very special woman in his life.

Uniquely special.

But she'd have to wait for his next entrance to know if that was true.

CHAPTER NINE

MEGAN'S assurances that she was okay with what had happened between them did little to relieve the turmoil in Johnny's mind. Her dismissive attitude had made him feel…unimportant to her, as though she'd only been using him to make herself feel better. Certainly she'd been closing the door on it, letting him know she wasn't expecting nor inviting a repeat performance.

Was wishing him well with the movie her way of putting him back in a pigeonhole that had nothing to do with her life? At least there'd been no scorn attached to it, more a straightforward acceptance that this was what he did. Nevertheless, even that seemed to emphasise the distance she seemed intent on establishing, telling him unequivocally that—*unlike him*—Gundamurra was *the only stage* for her.

Fair comment, Johnny told himself, though everything within him wanted to fight it. However, the current circumstances were wrong for making any headway on that ground. On any ground. And maybe *he* was wrong for her in any long-term sense. Johnny felt he couldn't be certain of anything until he returned to Gundamurra and put in a lot of time on the sheep station with Megan.

Back in Arizona, the movie wasn't fun anymore. He grew annoyed with the script, especially in the scenes he had to play with a rancher's widow. They didn't sit right with him. Neither did the ending. He kept thinking of how it would be for Megan if she were the widow, struggling to survive and having to make the choice of helping a cowboy who would inevitably leave her.

He argued with the director, insisting that the whole feel of the scenes was wrong, that they should be stark and powerful, pulsing with tension over the conflict of interests, not just some token female interest in the movie, and the cowboy should feel compelled to return to the ranch once his mission had been accomplished.

He won his point.

The female lead was very grateful to him for the meatier role. Too damned grateful, making a nuisance of herself. He had to explain he was seriously involved with another woman. What woman? she demanded to know, since there was none in evidence. Johnny kept his mouth shut, only too aware of what the media would do with a name. He couldn't bring that circus down on Megan, especially when there was nothing but a business partnership settled between them.

She kept her word, e-mailing him reports on what she was doing at Gundamurra, how his money was being used, accounting for every dollar put into the place. He both welcomed and hated her messages which were totally devoid of anything personal. It was as though the intimacy they had shared was a brief aberration, best forgotten.

He kept his own replies matter-of-fact, trying not to impinge on what she clearly saw as her authority, trying not to beg more interest in him from her. It was clear that what he was doing had no real existence in her life. He understood this but found it uncomfortably belittling. Was all he had achieved so *useless* to her mind?

He didn't mention the movie, apart from counting the schedule down—two more months, six weeks, four, two, a few more days. He didn't stay for the wrap-up party. He didn't care that the director seemed impressed with his acting ability. The moment he was no longer needed for any more scenes, contract fulfilled, he packed up and moved out, heading home to Gundamurra and Megan Maguire.

The land was in no better shape than when Johnny had last seen it—still no rain—but the sheep definitely were, Megan thought with satisfaction. There were more watering holes for them, thanks to the extra artesian bores his money had made possible, and the feed they were trucking in made a huge difference. Besides, she didn't anticipate any problems with Johnny over her management. His replies to her e-mailed reports had held nothing but approval.

Her only problems with him would be personal, and it was impossible to know how to handle them until she was with him again. She checked her watch as she headed towards the homestead kitchen for morning tea. Only a few more hours and he'd be flying in. Once he arrived…Megan told herself she had to remain calm, wait and see how he behaved towards her, keep reassessing the situation as she gathered more information.

She found Evelyn alone in the kitchen, vigorously grating carrot for Johnny's favourite cake. No doubt the housekeeper's two helpers, Brenda and Gail, were polishing up his guest suite, ensuring everything was in perfect readiness for his welcome home. Megan brushed off Evelyn's offer to make tea, munching some dry biscuits to settle her stomach while she brewed the tea herself. As soon as she sat down at the table with a steaming mugful, the grating stopped and Evelyn faced her with a determined air of confrontation.

'Are you going to tell him?'

Megan shrugged her bewilderment. 'Tell…whom… what?'

Evelyn wiped her hands on a cloth, the dark brown eyes of her aboriginal heritage measuring some goal she had in mind before speaking again. 'Don't think you can be fooling me, Miss Megan. I've seen the signs too many times.'

The nausea she'd been fighting every morning for weeks rolled around her stomach.

'Reckon I knew Miss Lara was pregnant even before she did,' Evelyn went on, leaving no doubt about the subject she was bent on tackling.

Megan realised it was useless to deny it. 'Have you told anyone?' she asked anxiously, alarmed at the thought that everyone on the station was aware of her condition and holding to a conspiracy of silence until she was ready to admit it.

'No. But I'll tell Mr Johnny if you don't,' came the challenging reply.

'You mustn't do that, Evelyn,' Megan instantly cried, panic welling up at the thought of any premature disclosure which might undermine her plans for the future.

'No good comes from keeping secrets that shouldn't be kept,' Evelyn bored in with absolute conviction. 'Especially from the man who fathered the child.'

'What makes you think Johnny's the father?' Megan shot back at her, desperate to raise enough doubt to give herself more time.

Evelyn clucked her contempt for any other possibility. 'No-one else it could be. Think I didn't know what you were up to...day of Mr Patrick's funeral...wanting to turn Mr Johnny's head? All these years...watching how you are with him? One way or another—nice or nasty—you've been set on making him take notice of you.'

Humiliation burned through her. Had her feelings been so horribly transparent to everyone? No, they couldn't have been, she frantically argued to herself. Johnny had believed she disliked him. Her sisters had been worried about her reaction to their father's will. They had simply been anxious that she not be hostile to Johnny and the help he could give. Mitch and Ric had taken that stance, too. Only Evelyn...Evelyn who cared about anything relating to Johnny...

'It's not his fault I'm pregnant,' Megan blurted out. 'It's not fair to load it on him.'

'Takes two to make a child,' came the firm rebuttal. 'Accepting the blame for it makes no difference, Miss Megan. The child belongs to him, as well as you.'

'I let him believe I was protected,' she pleaded. 'I'm the one who's responsible for this pregnancy. He would have ensured it didn't happen.'

Evelyn shook her head, disappointment and disapproval stamped on her expression. 'If you wove a web of lies to get Mr Johnny into your bed, you'll only make the situation worse with more lies. Time you faced up to yourself and to him.'

'I don't want him to feel trapped. That's not fair, Evelyn,' she repeated emphatically, gathering strength to fight any interference with whatever she decided to do.

'You think he'd want *his* child to be as fatherless as he was? No way, Miss Megan. No way. You just pile injustice on top of injustice if you keep this from him.' Her eyes narrowed in grim judgement. 'You're thinking of yourself. What you want. Always been that way. But I won't let you cut Mr Johnny out of what is rightfully his. You tell him or I will.'

'It's not your business!' It was a desperate cry of protest. This was between her and Johnny and she needed time to work out how best to approach the future…what arrangement to make with him.

Evelyn seemed to puff herself up with even more determination. 'Your dear mother's gone. Your father whom I admired and respected more than any other man on earth is gone.' She lifted a hand and shook a finger at Megan. 'They put me here. They trusted me to get things right. And neither of them would ever have planned to cheat a good man.'

Cheat…that was a totally unacceptable word. Megan recoiled from it. She'd been carrying a wretched load of guilt for weeks. That was nothing new. Yet mixed in with the guilt was an insidious streak of exhilarating pleasure in having Johnny Ellis's child—a part of him he couldn't take away from her. But *cheating* him…that didn't sit at all well.

Evelyn planted her hands on her ample hips. Her big bosom heaved. Her chin was thrust out in belligerent pride. 'I've lived at Gundamurra all my life. Over fifty years now. Served your parents best I could. Always followed their example. You can sack me if you want, Miss Megan. Your father gave you the right to do that…'

Gundamurra without Evelyn?

Shocking thought…even more shocking than cheating.

'…but as long as I'm here, I won't stand by and let you pull the wool over Mr Johnny's eyes, not on something as important as this will be to him. His child…'

Mine, too, Megan thought, fiercely possessive.

'You can't expect me to hit him with it the moment he steps off his plane,' she swiftly argued.

'You should have told him already,' came the damning retort. 'Every minute you leave it makes it worse. More underhand. More *unfair*,' she hammered home.

A relentless drive for truth was looking Megan straight in the face—impossible to ignore—impossible to even bend. Evelyn would serve Johnny with it along with her carrot cake if she was not satisfied with immediate action on this issue.

Strong loyalties had been stirred.

To Evelyn's mind, Patrick's daughter had not been acting as Patrick's daughter should, letting down the tradition of justice at Gundamurra, lying to a man who had learnt trust here, trusting her father, trusting himself. And perhaps the very longevity of her service did give her the right to feel she had to be the keeper of that trust, regardless of whether it served Megan's interests or not.

'I'm sorry you feel…so let down by me, Evelyn.'

She heaved a troubled sigh. 'It's your parents I'm thinking of, Miss Megan. They'd be telling you the same as I am. Lay it out in the open and deal with it.'

No other choice now.

'Tonight. I'll tell him tonight,' Megan promised.

Evelyn weighed that answer and finally conceded to it. 'I'll know tomorrow morning if you haven't done it,' she warned. 'Hard enough to look Mr Johnny in the face today, holding back what he should know.'

A brief reprieve.

At least she'd have a little time to gauge Johnny's attitude towards her, find out how long he intended to stay at Gundamurra this time, what career commitments he might have made while working on the movie, how much of his future was tied up elsewhere.

She'd wanted to feel prepared for every contingency before laying out the fact that would inevitably have a far ranging effect on the rest of their lives, wanted to have answers ready for whatever was Johnny's reaction to it.

However, Evelyn's words had stung her conscience. There was no denying the truth of them. Johnny would not want his child to be fatherless, as he himself had been. Which meant she had to share.

No cheating him out of the role he'd want to play—
a role he'd insist on playing.

Roles...exits and entrances...

What had she done in her own selfish desire to
have her needs answered?

One careless act.

A reckless lie.

Though even acknowledging she hadn't been fair
to Johnny, she couldn't regret doing it.

She *wanted* this child.

CHAPTER TEN

SOMETHING was wrong.

Even Evelyn's superb carrot cake with the cream cheese icing did not settle the churning in Johnny's stomach. Fair enough that Megan was tense about his homecoming, but never before had Evelyn been uncomfortable in his presence. Both women's responses to him seemed strained and they avoided eye contact with each other, focussing on him with a kind of forced eagerness to make him feel welcome, rushing to fill any brief silence with a host of questions about the movie, his trip, whether or not he'd stopped over in Sydney to see Ric and Mitch.

Something big was hidden in the silence they rushed to cover.

Trouble at Gundamurra?

Johnny had to force himself to eat the cake, drink the tea, all the time waiting for the axe to fall, whatever it was.

Weird how quickly everything could change. His heart had been dancing with pleasure when he landed. Megan had been standing by the Land Rover, waiting to drive him up to the homestead from the airstrip. Although a hat was jammed on her head, her glorious hair was loose, tumbling around her shoulders, surely a sign that she wanted to please him...as a woman.

Once he'd emerged from the plane, his legs had

eaten up the distance between them, every fast stride pumping with anticipation. But she'd thrust out a stiff, formal hand, and he'd felt constrained to hold back the pounding urge to hug her tight and keep holding her until the warm imprint of her body had assuaged the need to feel her flesh and blood reality again.

Her smile had been stiff, too.

Okay, let her get used to having me here again, he'd told himself. *Give her time to relax in my company.*

Now she was babbling on, trying to sound bright and natural while Evelyn was plying him with afternoon tea, her dark eyes empty of their normal sparkle at seeing him. He could feel the worry in their minds. It was like an invisible monster, growing bigger every minute, claws out ready to grab him, like the monsters of his childhood lurking in the cupboard his foster parents had used for punishing bad boys. He'd made up music in his head to drive them away, but no music was going to drive this away.

Finally he could stand it no longer.

Just as with Ric, holding the news of Patrick's death from him, Johnny could not wait for what he knew to be something bad. 'Tell me what's wrong!' he burst out in urgent demand.

It jolted them both into a silence that was clearly fraught with hidden concerns. No denial from either of them. The monster grew bigger in Johnny's mind.

Evelyn looked at Megan.

Megan had frozen into shocked stillness. Her hat was off now and even her vibrant hair was motionless, her grey eyes suddenly like opaque glass, nothing shining through.

'Evelyn…' he appealed.

The motherly housekeeper, who usually enjoyed indulging his every wish, shook her head, not even the hint of an appeasing smile on her face. 'It's not for me to say, Mr Johnny.' Grave, decisive words, accompanied by another anxious glance at Patrick's daughter, her employer.

There had always been a free and easy mood in Evelyn's kitchen. The heart of a home, Johnny had thought.

What had Megan done to change that?

Patrick wouldn't like it.

This wasn't how Gundamurra should feel.

Johnny instantly determined to change it back to what it should be. Whatever was going on had to be stopped, turned around.

Megan stirred out of her stunned state. His eyes bored into hers, demanding enlightenment. No way was he going to let her evade giving it. She might own fifty-one percent of Gundamurra but he had rights here, too.

'Let's go—' heat whooshed into her cheeks, vitality returning in an embarrassed rush '—to the office, Johnny.'

The office.

It was business then.

'Okay.' He could handle that.

He stood up.

Evelyn instantly busied herself at the sink, not looking at him, washing her hands, which Johnny couldn't help thinking was somehow symbolic.

Megan led off, leaving him to follow. Even when they reached the verandah that skirted the inner quadrangle of the homestead, she didn't pause to let him fall into step with her, marching on in a driven fashion, back straight, head high, not glancing at him when he caught up with her. He noted that her cheeks were still scorched with heat. And her hands were clenched. Whatever the problem was, she found it painful, being forced to impart it to him.

Pride badly hurt, he decided. Some huge mistake in managing Gundamurra. She'd hate to fail or be found wanting with anything to do with the sheep station. Whatever the crisis was, Johnny was determined to get around it, one way or another. Surely there was nothing that couldn't be fixed.

She didn't wait for him to lean past her and open the door to the office. She barged straight in, assuming he would follow and close the door behind them, which, of course, he did. It surprised him that she didn't go directly to her father's desk, take his chair, protect herself with some sense of authority. She veered off to stand over the chess table, hugging herself tightly as she stared down at the black and white battleground.

It was a stance that bristled with spiky tension, insisting on space around her. Johnny trod softly, moving over to the desk, propping himself against the front of it, trying to establish a relaxed, noncritical air. He hadn't come home to beat her over the head with anything. He wanted her trust. If she'd just place some confidence in him…but there was none forthcoming at the moment.

'It's okay,' he soothed. 'I'm not going to bite, Megan. Just tell me…'

Her head tilted back. She swung around to face him. Her expression seemed torn between intense inner conflict and a need to rise above it.

'I lied to you, Johnny.'

The bare statement held both guilt and defiance.

His mind clicked instantly to the e-mailed reports of what she'd done at Gundamurra. Had she baulked at using his money, after all? He hadn't checked, believing everything she'd told him. Surely she wouldn't have carried out such an elaborate deceit. From the air, the vast sheep station had still looked drought-stricken, but since there'd been no rain, he hadn't expected to actually *see* a difference. Tomorrow, he'd thought, she would show him.

'What did you lie about?' he asked, doing his utmost to keep calm.

Her lashes fell. Her mouth twitched into a rueful grimace. She took a deep breath, forced herself to meet his gaze squarely, then laid it out. 'The night we spent together…I told you I was protected…and I wasn't.'

It took him several moments to unscramble his mind which had been totally focussed on possible problems at Gundamurra. Then it took several more moments for the implication of her words to sink in. The shock of it robbed him of any ready speech.

'I'm pregnant,' she shot at him in case he hadn't put it together.

Right! he thought, still unable to produce a verbal response. He simply stared at her as understanding flooded through his mind. Evelyn knew. No hiding a three-month pregnancy from Evelyn. She'd known about Lara's pregnancy. Probably remembered his reaction to that piece of news, too, letting Ric know immediately so his old friend understood Lara's position and could act on it if he wanted to.

Evelyn would have advised Megan that Johnny had to be told. But what did Megan want of him?

That was the big question.

Though instantly overriding it was *what he wanted*.

Megan was pregnant with his child.

There was no question about what should be done.

'We get married,' he said, pushing off the desk to stand tall and determined against any opposition she threw at him.

'Married,' she repeated, as though she couldn't believe he had made that leap.

'I think Mitch told me it can't be done under a month. We can fly to Bourke tomorrow, sign whatever papers have to be signed for legal notice…'

'Johnny, people don't get married over a pregnancy anymore,' she cried, her arms unfolding, hands flapping in agitation. 'Especially when…'

'It was just a night of sex?' he finished for her, all his doubts about Megan's motivation for that night crowding into his mind.

He watched her flounder, so many emotions flitting across her face, it was impossible to decipher what she was thinking. Johnny decided it didn't matter. The only important end to this conversation was to give the child she was carrying—*his child*—the kind of security every child deserved to have.

'Look!' she finally pleaded. 'I did something stupid…wilful…'

'We're all guilty of rash acts from time to time, Megan,' he said sympathetically.

'I'm responsible for the consequences, not you, Johnny,' she shot back at him.

'That's beside the point. Whether planned or not, I'm the father of this child,' he stated simply.

'It doesn't mean you have to marry me.' Wild pride in her eyes.

'Do you have a problem with being my wife?'

No answer.

Anguished uncertainty in her eyes.

The sex between them had been good, Johnny argued to himself. She couldn't deny that. And he was co-owner of Gundamurra. Difficult for her to marry some outsider when she had a child by the man who would continue to share her home.

'I'm here, Megan,' he pressed. 'You can't send me away. I'm not going away. Why not accept—'

'But you *will* go away,' she broke in vehemently. 'You always do. Career opportunities will come up…'

'I don't have to take them. I can afford to retire from the whole entertainment circus right now.'

'You won't want to. Not in the long run.'

'Don't tell me what I want, Megan. More than anything I want to be a good father.'

'You don't have to be married to fulfil that role, Johnny.'

'You'd prefer us to be single parents?' His mind buzzed around what advantage Megan might see in that situation and zeroed in on the worst possible scenario. Connected to her insistent belief that he would go away… 'If I have to fight you for custody rights, I will,' he fired at her in grim challenge. 'Just because you're the mother doesn't make you the arbiter of what's best for our child.'

She looked appalled. 'You wouldn't drag him— her—around the world with you.'

'Why not? Gundamurra might be the centre of your universe, but would a fair judge rule that a child can't experience anything else? If you don't want to be my wife and work at being a harmonious couple…'

'A good father would want a stable life for his child,' she fiercely argued.

'Yes. And also want the child to feel loved by both parents. Not one cutting out the other. Was that what you intended to do with me, Megan? Cut me out?'

'No!' She paced around, pumped up with too much turbulent energy to remain still, though her arms folded across her chest again, projecting a need for self-containment, excluding him by action if not by word.

Johnny kept his distance, watching her deal with the pressure he had mounted for the outcome he wanted. Anger was still burning through him. If she had imagined he'd just waltz off about his business and leave her to bring up their child any way she wanted, she could certainly dismiss that idea right now.

She paused, shooting him a measuring look. 'You said Gundamurra was home to you. I want it to be home to our child, too.'

'So why not make us a family, Megan? What objection do you have to marrying me?'

'If I marry you…will you leave our son or daughter here with me when you take on career commitments overseas?'

Johnny knew that being a hands-on father would always come first with him. However, his career was clearly a big stumbling block to Megan, had been for a long time and still was, though he'd thought he'd answered the prejudices she'd held about it. The arrangement she wanted to put into place seemed very one-sided to him, and certainly not to his liking.

'Should I take on work that requires me to be elsewhere, I would want my family to go with me.'

'No!' Scarlet pride in her cheeks. 'I will not compete with…' Her mouth clamped shut, but her eyes held a violent storm of feeling.

'Compete with what?' he probed.

'The women in your world,' she flung at him, hating having to say it yet unable to hold it in.

He shook his head. The absurdity was…*she* was the only woman he wanted. Nevertheless, the realisation finally dawned that Megan was consumed by an intense sense of vulnerability, fighting him to keep herself and their child on the only secure ground she knew.

'There is no competition,' he said gently, wanting to erase her fears.

Rank disbelief stared back at him.

It propelled him forward, his hands spread in an openly inviting gesture. 'You *can* trust me, Megan. As my wife, you'll have my absolute commitment and loyalty.'

Still the rigid stance, arms folded in stubborn resistance, but there was a wavering in her eyes, perhaps a wanting to believe that couldn't quite be suppressed.

He curved his hands over the tense muscles of her shoulders. 'I promise you Gundamurra will always be our home, the big constant in our lives. But if I ask you to leave it sometimes, to share something else with me for a while, aren't you brave enough to try that, Megan?'

'*This* is my life, Johnny. You can't expect me to leave it. I don't want to be a fish out of water. I'd hate it.'

His hands instinctively slid up to cup her face, forcing her gaze to hold his while he pushed for a resolution. 'This is fear talking, Megan. And what we need here is a leap of faith. The reality is we're going to have a child. We should live together as a family. And marriage is about giving to each other, not laying down conditions that will limit—if not wreck—the relationship we should have as husband and wife. I'm not even asking you to meet me halfway. Just give a little. At least...give it a chance.'

He dropped his hands and backed off. 'Think about it. My position is not going to change. Either we get married and we both try to make it work as best we can...or I'll fight you for my fair share of fatherhood. I won't be kept dangling on this, Megan. You have until tomorrow morning to decide.'

Johnny left the ultimatum hanging and walked to the door. As far as he was concerned, there was nothing more to discuss. Whichever way Megan chose, his own course was clear. His child was going to

have the kind of father he would have wanted himself—a father like Patrick—always there for him. Or
her. If Megan didn't ever come to love him, at least
their child would. No way was he going to miss out
on that!

'Wait!'

His hand was already on the doorknob when her
call whipped through the tense silence, halting his
exit. Johnny gritted his teeth and half-turned, conceding a few more moments but not prepared to enter
into further argument.

She'd dropped the folded arm posture and her
hands were now fretting at each other, revealing how
very nervous she was. Her eyes held a fearful pleading that he found painful. He'd never done anything
to hurt her. Never would. Her throat moved in a convulsive swallow, as though her thoughts sickened
her.

'Dammit, Megan!' he muttered fiercely. 'Can't
you see...?'

'I'll give it a chance.'

'Give what a chance?'

'I'll marry you.'

CHAPTER ELEVEN

'WILL you, Megan Mary Maguire, take this man…'

While the marriage celebrant intoned the traditional vow with all due solemnity, Megan was still struggling to believe it was really happening, that she was standing here in full bridal regalia, about to say the words that would make her Johnny Ellis's wife.

This man… the one she'd always wanted… her wedding to him more a teenage fantasy than an adult reality, yet here they were, standing on the green grass of the inner quadrangle, everyone who worked on the homestead in attendance along with her family and Johnny's closest friends, bearing witness to the marriage. This was how she'd dreamed of it, although her father should have still been alive, giving her away.

Perhaps he was in spirit.

Certainly it was his will that had started the very personal situation between her and Johnny rolling. If only the baby hadn't forced this end, if she'd been sure of Johnny's love for her, Megan knew she might have been a deliriously happy bride. As it was, her stomach was full of butterflies and all she could do was hope that everything would turn out right. Or right enough to live with this decision.

The celebrant looked expectantly at her.

'I will,' she said.

A leap of faith.

'Will you, Johnny Ellis, take this woman…'

No doubt about his reply. He'd been the driving force towards this wedding from the moment she'd agreed to marry him. No quick civil ceremony in a register office. A proper celebration of their union in front of those closest to them. At Gundamurra, because it was the most appropriate location—home to both of them—and it would keep the wedding contained and private. Ric would do the photographs, some of which would be released to the media afterwards, making the marriage publicly known.

At first, she had protested the idea of a photo of her—Johnny Ellis's bride—being splashed around the world, becoming part of the publicity machine that surrounded his career. His reply had made any argument impossible—

'I'm not going to hide you, Megan. And I am not entering you into a competition. To me you are the most beautiful woman in the world and I want other women to know it. To know I'm married to you.'

She'd never thought of herself as beautiful. Not anything like the celebrities he had mixed with socially. Had he said that simply to quell the panic she felt at being compared to *them?* Whatever the truth, Megan had desperately wanted to live up to Johnny's stated view of her, at least on their wedding day.

She'd asked Ric's wife, Lara, who'd once been an international model, to help her choose the wedding dress, a fabulous design in ivory silk with lace and seed pearls, making it possible to wear the pearl necklace, and a wonderful long veil attached to a pearl tiara.

Evelyn, with sentimental tears in her eyes, had declared she looked just like a princess, and her dear mother and father would be very proud of her today, but most of all Megan wanted Johnny to be proud of her, proud to have her as his wife.

'I will,' he said, very firmly.

Then they were exchanging the gold rings he had chosen. She was glad he wanted to wear one, too, the symbol of his commitment to their marriage.

This past month he'd devoted most of his time to catching up on all the work being done at Gundamurra, proving to her that he had a deep interest in it, even making suggestions for improvements that should be considered when the climate was right. But how long would he stay here before his career called him away? And how was she going to cope with his life?

Don't think about it.

Not today.

'I now pronounce you husband and wife.'

Johnny was smiling at her.

She could hear the clicking of Ric's camera.

Her heart was rocketing around her chest in anticipation of the kiss that was to come. It was impossible to move her facial muscles into a responding smile. Her mind was wildly sorting out the expression in Johnny's eyes. Pleasure in her appearance, yes. Also a flash of triumphant satisfaction, possibly in having carried through what he'd decided was right, even to holding off having any intimate connection with her until their wedding night. But mostly, she saw a simmering desire, revelling in the promise that she was his, to have and to hold from this day forth.

Sweet relief.

At least he did want sex with her.

He kissed her with a slow, seductive sensuality, his mouth certainly seeming to suggest that passion was just lying in wait for the privacy of their honeymoon. No problems in bed, Megan assured herself. Maybe her pregnancy actually made her more desirable to him. She hoped so, acutely conscious of the more rounded tummy hidden by the clever design of her wedding gown.

He steered her to the table where they were to sign the marriage certificate. Once that was done, everyone came up to congratulate them, wishing them a long and happy life together.

It amazed Megan how genuinely given these sentiments were, as though no doubts about the success of this marriage were being harboured. They knew she was pregnant. Neither she nor Johnny had tried to keep that a secret. Yet it seemed irrelevant to them. It was as though they had all decided that this match had been made in heaven and it met with their heartfelt approval.

Whether Ric or Mitch had raised any questions with Johnny, she didn't know. They gave no sign of it. Her sisters had thought it marvellous that Johnny wanted to marry her. Not one hint of criticism from them. Apparently they were perfectly confident that a workable future could be achieved between the two of them, probably on the principle that love conquers all.

Except the only *love* Megan was sure of was Johnny's love for their unborn child.

A huge barbecue dinner had been organised. Fairy

lights had been strung around the pepper trees, just as they always were for Christmas, and the mood was just as merry. Speeches were made. Johnny played his guitar and sang a song he'd composed especially for her. He called it 'Coming Home' and everyone was moved by it, including Megan, who fiercely wished that the lyrics were a true expression of how he felt, not merely a string of effective sentiments that stirred emotions.

It prompted Lara to ask if he'd sing at a charity concert which was being organised in Sydney, all the proceeds to be used for drought relief, wherever it was most needed. 'Your name would pull in more people, Johnny,' she pressed. 'The concert won't be for a couple of more months. We have to fix a date for all the artists we want to be available. The idea is for them to donate their talent for the cause.'

'I'm taking time out from that scene, Lara,' he excused apologetically.

Because of me, Megan instantly thought. 'It's okay, Johnny,' she leapt in. 'I won't mind if you do it.'

He frowned at her, puzzled by her apparent eagerness for him to move back into the limelight.

'It will help people who are in desperate need of help,' she rushed out, needing him to see she could be fair.

'Lara said the concert will be held in a couple of months, Megan,' he reminded her, still frowning over her impulsive urging. 'I won't want to leave you at home alone at that point in time, being so pregnant, possibly needing my help.'

Was he worried about the baby? She'd only be six

or seven months along, dependent on the date of the concert. Her pregnancy would definitely be showing by then, but Johnny had said he had no intention of *hiding* her.

'I could go with you,' she argued, determined not to appear selfish. Besides, this performance was to be staged in Australia, not overseas, and should only take up a week or two with rehearsals. 'It will give me the chance to buy baby things in Sydney,' she added eagerly.

'And I can guide you to the best shops,' Lara offered with her lovely smile. 'We'll have great fun shopping, Megan.'

'I'll come with you,' Kathryn chimed in, smiling at Mitch who was proudly carrying around their new baby son. 'Josh will be needing bigger clothes by then.'

'The mothers' club,' Johnny commented with an indulgent shake of his head.

'Yes. And I can just see you and Mitch and Ric forming the fathers' club in the not too distant future,' Kathryn retorted laughingly.

'You could be right,' he acknowledged.

If he really did base himself in Australia from now on, Megan thought hopefully.

'About the concert, Lara,' he went on. 'Send me the paperwork on it and I'll let you know.'

No promise.

Megan was disappointed that she hadn't won his approval. She silently resolved to find out what his reservations were about committing himself. There was still so much about Johnny she didn't know, despite having known him for most of her life.

But he was, without a doubt, the most handsome man in the world to her, breathtakingly so in his formal black dinner suit. And now, for better or for worse, he was her husband. Megan told herself to stop worrying about the future and just concentrate on tonight, being with him in every sense.

Tomorrow they were flying to Broome for a week's honeymoon—a week of making love and sharing intimate thoughts, she hoped. Tonight she wanted to convince Johnny that it wasn't *just sex* for her, banishing any thought that she'd only been *using* him to make herself feel better on the night of her father's wake.

She wanted *him.*

Only him.

She tried to transmit this while Ric was posing them for the photograph he'd envisaged being the definitive one of their wedding. It was late in the evening—time for the party to break up—and everyone had followed Ric out to the setting he had chosen, away from all the buildings. He stood Megan and Johnny facing each other, holding hands. Behind them was a dark empty landscape, seemingly flat to the horizon, above it the brilliant stars of the outback sky.

They had to wait for him to get the lighting just right. Johnny joked about the exacting eye of an artist but he seemed happy to co-operate with his old friend's concept.

'That sure beats a cathedral,' Mitch murmured, almost reverently, looking up at the canopy of stars. 'Now I know why you won all those photography prizes, Ric.'

'To me, nature always beats anything man-made,' Ric answered. 'And this shot is meant to be totally primal, the imprint of greatest human faith in each other against the stark might of the outback.'

A convulsive little shiver ran through Megan at the all too perceptive truth of those words.

Johnny squeezed her hands, instantly imparting warmth and strength. She looked up into eyes that blazed their searing message into her heart...*believe in me*. She didn't hear the camera click that captured her own surge of emotion, the huge welling of need and desire to believe their marriage would survive anything life threw at them. Survive and thrive here at Gundamurra, because this was where she belonged, where she wanted Johnny to feel he belonged, with her and the children they would have.

Home...

And that overwhelming wave of feeling was still sweeping through her when they were finally alone together in the room where their baby had been conceived. She was no longer nervous, nor apprehensive, nor worried about convincing Johnny of anything. A blissful sense of union with him permeated every kiss, every touch, building a deep passion for all the intense pleasure they could give to each other.

They were married.

On this—their wedding night—all other realities were left to be met when they had to be met.

CHAPTER TWELVE

THE honeymoon was pure sensual bliss—a week of hot days and balmy nights in Broome—time out from the drought problems at Gundamurra—nothing to do but enjoy themselves in any way impulse took them.

Megan found that sexual pleasure with Johnny was extremely addictive. He was a marvellous lover and there was certainly no doubting his desire for her. It seemed to constantly simmer in his eyes, flaring into passion when she dared to provoke it, and twinkling with wicked satisfaction when she lay contentedly in his arms afterwards.

Though occasionally she felt a stab of jealousy at the look of entranced love on his face when he felt the baby move. Not once did he speak of loving her, and Megan could not bring herself to admit to the feelings she'd always had about him. She was the mother of his child. That was what their marriage was based on. And Johnny certainly did his best to be a husband she could be happy with.

And she *was* happy for the most part. When they returned to Gundamurra, Johnny threw himself into working with the sheep, going out with the men to do whatever chores were scheduled, coming home to her each evening with the air of a man well satisfied with jobs done. She couldn't fault his commitment to their partnership. The only problem that arose between them centred on the charity concert Lara had mentioned on their wedding day.

The paperwork had been sent for Johnny to peruse. Megan fretted over his reluctance to make a positive decision, acutely conscious that her negative reaction to his career might be at the root of his aversion to the idea. Wanting to make amends for her previous attitude, she kept pressing him, reasoning that drought relief was the best possible cause for donating his talent, and very appropriate since he was now personally connected to the land.

She did not foresee that the agreement she finally won from him would almost immediately throw them into conflict. A request for a publicity interview at Gundamurra came in and Johnny was strongly opposed to granting it.

'You said you weren't going to hide me,' Megan argued.

'It's not hiding you. It's protecting you,' Johnny argued back. 'You've had no experience of dealing with the media. Anything you say can be skewed to fit into the story an interviewer wants to do.'

'But I'm a first-hand authority on the drought.'

'They won't be after a story on the drought.'

She didn't believe him.

She suspected he didn't want to expose her to his career so soon after their marriage. Yet to her mind, it had to be faced, and the sooner it stopped being a hurdle to be avoided, the better. Besides, a story on how the drought was affecting Gundamurra would surely make city people more aware of the problems in the country. How could it possibly hurt her? What was he protecting her from?

'You can't control what people write, Megan,' he stated, impatient with her stubbornness on this issue. 'The only kind of interview you can control is on live television, and it takes a lot of practice to get that right, believe me.'

All she could see was he didn't want to share this part of his life with her. Johnny Ellis was the star, the crowd-puller. She was just his wife in the background.

To close the rift that had opened up between them, Johnny gave way on granting the interview at Gundamurra. The story was subsequently headlined—The Outback Bridal Rescue—with a half page photograph of Ric's special shot of them on their wedding night.

The only comment on the drought was that without Johnny Ellis's investment in Gundamurra, even this well-established sheep station would not have survived it. The rest of it was about Johnny's career and speculation about its future now that he was supposedly married to the land. Or was he simply carrying over the cowboy role he'd played in the movie which was yet to be released, in real life for a while?

Megan hated it—hated the doubts it raised in her mind, hated the way every *important* thing she and Johnny had spoken about had been virtually ignored.

'How do you live with this?' she raged.

'Megan, you chose to let them invade our privacy here, to let yourself be exploited. Will you listen to me now?' he answered quietly.

She listened.

He laid out his plan, explained the reasons for it and Megan ended up feeling she had no choice but to accede to it, given that she was pregnant and Johnny's schedule would be hectic with rehearsals and handling the media coverage expected of him to get maximum publicity for the concert.

So here she was, being mollycoddled by Ric and Lara in their lovely home at Balmoral Beach, while Johnny held court from a top-class city hotel with top-class security guarding him from unwanted attention, escorting him to and from wherever he had to be.

She went shopping with Lara and Kathryn, unaccosted by anyone. She had the freedom of the city to enjoy in any way she liked, with good company readily available. Except it wasn't Johnny's company. And it was lonely in bed at night.

Johnny called her on his mobile phone frequently. She could hardly complain he was excluding her from his life, yet she did feel excluded. Mostly they talked about what she'd been doing, where she'd been, what she'd bought. It seemed to her he deliberately minimised his activities, perhaps believing they would be of no interest to her. Even when she pressed him on them he was dismissive, not allowing her any sense of sharing.

'Will it always be like this?' she cried in exasperation during one call. 'You there, me here?'

It evoked a silence that suddenly crawled with black irony. This was what she had initially wanted, to have no part of his career, for her and their child to occupy a separate place in his life. But now Megan was desperate to believe that the intimacy they had forged during the past two months together at

Gundamurra *could* be transplanted elsewhere. Or didn't Johnny believe that was possible?

She cursed the narrowness of her previous attitude, worrying that it was still casting a shadow on Johnny's thinking, despite her attempts to show him it was different now. Her nerves tightened up as she waited for his reply, wanting him to say something she could get her teeth into and tear apart.

'No. You won't always be pregnant, Megan.' Strained patience in his voice, making her feel like a petulant child. 'As I've already explained to you, I just want to save you unnecessary stress in your condition. It will only be another week and we'll be home again. Okay?'

Eminently reasonable.

But in Megan's already stressed mind it translated to Johnny's judgement that she wouldn't cope with the demands of his career and he didn't want the hassle of looking after her, having to mop up her inexperienced errors of judgement which made her more a hindrance than a help, especially when he should be focussing on putting his best professional foot forward.

I'm being selfish again, she told herself, and let the issue drop, privately vowing to learn how to handle his world better the next time around, listening to him instead of barging forward with her own ideas.

Yet Johnny's emphasis on her pregnancy kept niggling—the child who meant so much to him. Megan couldn't help thinking he wouldn't choose to be in a hotel room by himself if the baby had been born. He'd want *his family* with him. And while their marriage might have seemed reasonably safe and solid while living together at Gundamurra, maybe she'd been living in a fool's paradise and deep unbridgeable gaps could open up at any moment.

Ric and Lara were indulgently amused by her desire to watch Johnny's spot on each television show that featured him, to listen to the talk-back radio programs he participated in, to read every interview printed in the newspapers. They thought she was besotted with her new husband. The truth was her secret insecurities compelled her to know precisely how Johnny performed, whether *she* was mentioned and what Johnny said about her and their marriage.

For the most part he diverted any questions about his private life, speaking with surprising passion about the plight of farmers and pastoralists, many of whom had worked the land for generations, benefiting all Australians. He reminded people of all the traditional poetry and songs that epitomised the hardships of country life, the culture of survival that was at the core of our patriotism.

'You've got to hand it to Johnny. He hits straight at the heart,' Ric commented appreciatively, while they were watching him perform on one current affairs program.

Yes, right at the heart of the anchorwoman who was interviewing him, Megan thought, watching the body language that shouted how very attractive she found him in every sense. And he was...charming, sincere, his voice an incredibly seductive tool, and all of him emanating so much sexual magnetism, the woman was turning into a melting marshmallow instead of living up to her reputation for being sharp and tough.

It left Megan with the certainty that he could have married anyone, but didn't have to. They'd fall at his feet, anyway. It was only because she was having his child that he'd decided to marry her. All his love-making, caring... If she hadn't been pregnant, would he have given so much? Any of it?

On that one fateful night of sex, he would have used protection.

Now he was protecting *her condition.*

Protecting his fatherhood.

Megan's emotions were in a total mess by the time the night of the concert arrived. Lara, who was on the charity committee, had obtained tickets for what she considered the prime position in the Sydney Entertainment Centre. They were in the front row of the central tier of seats facing the stage.

'Above the floor level,' she explained, 'with a barrier between us and any madness that might break out.'

'Madness?' Megan queried.

'You've never been to a pop concert, Megan?'

'No, I haven't.'

'The area closest to the stage is usually called the mosh pit. Fans can totally spin out, especially when the music gets them going. We'll be safe where our seats are situated.'

Safe...that word grated on Megan's jangling nerves. Yet when they did take their seats in the huge auditorium which was jam-packed with thousands of people all buzzing with excited anticipation, she appreciated the choice Lara had made. Even more so when the first pop band onstage swung into action and the sound assault of their music was increased by almost incessant screaming from fans jumping up and down and carrying on like lunatics.

It was certainly an education to Megan about Johnny's life. She knew he'd done many concert tours throughout his career, more in the U.S.A. than here in Australia. He was a megastar on the country and western music scene, though his popularity was not limited to only those fans. His songs had universal appeal, which was why he was billed as the star act tonight, the last one onstage, bringing the concert to an end, leaving everyone happy and uplifted.

Clearly the performers got a huge kick out of the wildly enthusiastic response from their audience. Their energy level was amazing and there was certainly a sexual buzz in their strutting. Was all this adulation addictive? Would someone who was used to it find life boringly flat without regular doses of it?

As the evening's entertainment progressed, security guards had to stop some fans from climbing onto the stage. Others had to be carried away for medical attention, having fainted from the crush or their own hyperexcitement.

Just before Johnny was to make his appearance, a girl with long blonde hair and a tight scarlet mini-dress was actually tossed by her companions onto the stage and she thrust a note into the retiring singer's hand before leaping off to escape the guards.

'Groupie,' Lara drily remarked. 'No doubt she'll

want to be picked out from the crowd backstage once the show is over.'

Megan was relieved the girl hadn't targeted Johnny.

Not that he'd be swayed by it. His view of groupies had convinced her that he would never take that kind of sexual advantage from his celebrity. She simply didn't need any more evidence of how desirable he was to other women. As it was, her nerves were on edge, waiting for his performance—live—in front of this massive crowd of people.

Definitely my last concert, Johnny thought grimly, waiting for the guys to vacate the stage. They were still prancing around, all pumped up from the wild response to their music, eating up the frenetic crowd energy while they could. The buzz didn't last. After the adrenaline rush came the let-down because it was all about the music and the event itself, not the person. Johnny knew he didn't want this anymore. Especially not the empty hotel room afterwards.

Tomorrow he could go home with Megan. To Gundamurra where he was genuinely liked for the man he was. Put all this artificial *love* behind him and raise a family where the love would be real. Megan would be happy about that. It was just too difficult for her to be faced with everything celebrity involved.

'Something for you, Johnny.' A photograph was thrust into his hand by the main vocalist of the band, now bouncing off stage. The guy winked at him. 'Blonde bomb in a red mini-dress, front row. Great tits.'

Johnny was about to toss it away when the guy added in a mocking drawl, 'Oh yeah! Said to tell you she was your long-lost sister. Try anything, some chicks.'

Sister!

The idea thumped into Johnny's heart.

It had never occurred to him that his mother might have had another child. He couldn't remember one but he didn't recall anything about that time. And he certainly hadn't been told he had a sister somewhere. But would he have been informed if the child had been adopted out? Maybe a baby. Which meant she'd be thirty-six now.

He stared at the photograph. Definitely not a teenager. Could be in her thirties. Difficult to tell a woman's age. He saw no likeness to himself but that meant nothing. She would have had a different father.

Long-lost sister... His stomach started churning. He'd never thought to do a search himself, believing he'd been the only one left abandoned by his mother's death.

What if he wasn't?

'Your turn to wow 'em, Johnny,' one of the backstage guys prompted him.

He heard the MC doing the introduction.

There was nowhere to stash the photograph except under his shirt. He caught sight of writing on the back as he turned it over to slide it down his V-neckline.

Please let me get to you—your sister, Jodie Ellis.

Jodie...Johnny...

Had she tried before and been turned away by his minders?

Or was it simply a groupie scam?

No time to think about it now.

He was on.

Blonde in a red mini-dress. Front row.

Megan was totally stunned by Johnny's performance. The screaming of the fans stopped the moment he began to sing. He just seemed to command the rapt attention of everyone in the auditorium, his strong, beautiful voice carrying waves of emotion that swept out and grabbed people by the throat.

He didn't need to gyrate around the stage. He didn't need to whip up excitement. He simply stood and delivered and there were sighs of pleasure as people swayed to his rhythm, happy clapping with the upbeat songs, thunderous applause when he finished each number and flashed the charismatic smile that would have charmed love out of a stone.

Megastar.

Of course, the fact that he was spectacularly male—a man's man—a woman's man—added immeasurably to his powerful attraction. Megan couldn't help noticing the blonde in the scarlet mini-dress doing everything she could to draw Johnny's attention to her. Apparently she had changed her mind about the main object of her desire tonight. No contest, Megan thought, but she didn't like it.

She particularly didn't like the fact that Johnny seemed distracted by the woman, his gaze returning to her again and again throughout his performance.

What was she doing that Megan couldn't see? Why was Johnny zeroing in on her so much?

It stirred up all the insecurities Megan was struggling with, especially since she couldn't make eye contact with him herself. Impossible for Johnny to actually see her so far back from the brilliantly lit stage. The major part of the audience had to be a dark blur to him, simply a presence he heard and felt and responded to.

At least he *knew* she was here, with his old friends and their wives. When he announced his final song, he did look directly to where they were seated and it gave Megan considerable relief to hear him say he'd composed this song for his wife on their wedding day—a very public acknowledgement of their marriage.

He already had the audience completely in his hands, but his rendition of 'Coming Home' was incredibly moving, heart-tugging, so much so that there were several moments of poignant silence at the end of it before the crowd erupted into huge prolonged applause, everyone on their feet, clapping, shouting, not wanting to let him leave the stage.

But with a simple hand salute to the crowd, he walked off and did not return. The audience eventually accepted that the concert was over. People started to move towards the exits, still buzzing with pleasure despite not having persuaded Johnny into an encore.

Megan would have been happy to leave, too, but she caught sight of a security guard escorting the troublesome blonde with an air of set purpose. The action unsettled her again. Lara, Kathryn, Ric, and

Mitch were enthusing over Johnny's performance as they all moved out to the aisle, ready to make their way out of the massive entertainment centre, but Megan was too distracted to voice any sensible comment herself.

'Can we go backstage?' she asked, impelled to settle the nagging sense of not knowing what was going on with Johnny, needing to be with him.

It wasn't planned.

But they went.

And were ushered into a dressing-room where the blonde in the scarlet mini-dress had her arms wound around Johnny's neck and her body plastered to his!

CHAPTER THIRTEEN

SHOCK held them all silent.

Except for the blonde.

Megan burned with humiliation as the woman rubbed her body provocatively, invitingly, against Johnny's and babbled on about how fantastic he was and she'd do anything—*anything* he wanted—just to be with him.

A blatant groupie.

And Johnny had to have given instructions for her to be brought to him.

Well, he was certainly caught in a spotlight now!

Yet there was no guilt on his face.

With an air of grim self-containment, he reached up and forcibly pulled down the arms that held him, stepping back out of body contact as he spoke with biting distaste. 'You picked the wrong mark.'

'But you sent for me,' the blonde protested.

No escape from that truth.

Megan's heart died.

If she hadn't come backstage, seen this for herself...

'Please...just go.' Johnny nodded to Megan. 'My wife is here.'

The blonde whipped around to see. Her gaze skated over the group who'd entered, fastened on Megan, raked her from head to foot in angry frustration, pausing at the now obvious bump of her pregnancy. 'So, you got him with that trap,' she said nastily.

'Go!' Johnny thundered, as though he could barely tolerate the offence, his expression fighting both pain and fury.

Trap was right, Megan thought miserably.

Having realised there was no choice but to accept defeat, the blonde flounced around them to the open doorway, jeeringly tossing back, 'You don't know what you're missing, Johnny.'

A stony pride settled on his face as he muttered, 'I do. I know exactly what I'm missing.' But he spoke to empty space. The blonde was gone. And his eyes had emptied of all feeling, too. There was suddenly a sense of dreadful emptiness permeating the whole room.

No-one spoke.

Megan sensed they were all hanging out for an acceptable explanation, possibly embarrassed at being witnesses to a scene none of them liked. Her hand instinctively moved to spread over the hump which held her baby, a fierce protective love welling up and choking her.

Wretched thoughts jumbled through her mind. There'd been no need for Johnny to marry her. She hadn't asked him to. Nor had she wanted him to feel he was missing out on anything. She hated that he did. How could she hold him to their marriage, knowing it got in the way of...*his life?*

Johnny visibly regathered himself and flashed a derisive look at Ric and Mitch. 'She claimed to be my long-lost sister.'

As though *they* would understand.

Not his wife.

'I thought…it was possible,' he added with a grimace that somehow expressed a world of loss.

A sister? Megan's mind whirled, trying to fit this idea into the train of circumstances she had watched, trying to understand how Johnny could have believed such an unlikely claim…what it might have meant to him.

'We're your family, Johnny,' Mitch said quietly.

'You'll always have us,' Ric backed up.

The three men…who'd been boys at Gundamurra…a brotherhood…but not linked by blood.

Johnny nodded, acknowledging the bond between them, yet his eyes were still bleak as his gaze fastened on the hand Megan had placed over her tummy and she intuitively knew what he was thinking. This baby was the only blood link to him…flesh of his flesh. No sister. But he would have a son or a daughter.

It was her baby, too, but she didn't think that counted to him. He wanted this child. Regardless of the cost to himself on any other level, *he needed to have this child in his life,* filling a hole she could not really imagine because she'd never been in his situation. Mitch had a sister and a son. Ric had a son and a daughter. Johnny was still alone in the world in any biological sense.

'Will you come back to the hotel with me tonight?' he asked her, a hollow quality in his voice that seemed to expect nothing, just a yes or no.

'Yes,' she said, all her nerves knotted with apprehension, yet the need to know what was on his mind was paramount—how their marriage really was for him, good or bad. He could put all his willpower behind a commitment, but feelings were something else.

He heaved a tired sigh. 'Ric, Mitch...' A wry appreciation flitted into a brief curl of his mouth. 'Good of you to be here for me, but...' He gestured an apologetic appeal.

'We'll leave you to it,' Mitch swiftly interpreted.

'Don't let this get you down, Johnny,' Ric quietly advised. 'We have to let the past go.'

'Guess it got up and bit me tonight, Ric.' He shrugged. 'Took me off guard. I'll be okay.'

He made a dismissive gesture and his two old friends moved out, taking their wives with them, closing the door to give him privacy with Megan.

Feeling totally ill-equipped to deal with emotions Johnny had never revealed to her, and painfully aware that she had not been invited backstage, she couldn't bring herself to go to him. Hopelessly tongue-tied, she stayed where she was, waiting for some sign that he actually welcomed her being here. Although he'd asked her to stay, the request had been made in front of others and might only have been some kind of test for loyalty from her, trust in his word.

Johnny seemed to be viewing her from a great distance, perhaps weighing her silence, her stillness, perhaps seeing a chasm between them that he didn't have the energy to cross. Was it up to her? Panic seized her mind, inducing a terrible torment of indecisiveness.

Finally he spoke, his mouth taking on an ironic

twist. 'I guess you thought it was something different.'

Megan inwardly writhed over the doubts and suspicions that had driven her backstage to check what was true or not. After what had just unfolded here she couldn't confess to them. It felt too wrong. As though it might be the end of any possible relationship between them if she did. Yet she had to say something. He had surely noticed her shock on seeing him with the blonde.

With a helpless little gesture of appeal she weakly offered, 'I'm sorry, Johnny. It looked…'

'As though I'd lied to you,' he drily finished for her. 'I haven't, Megan. Not about anything.'

He turned and picked up a photograph from the make-up bench behind him. 'This was passed to me by the singer who came offstage just before I went on. I would have tossed it away, but for what was written on the back.'

He held it out to her, making her feel forced to step forward and take it, forced to read the words that had swayed him into checking out the woman who had claimed to be *his long-lost sister*. She looked just as tarty in the photograph as she had in real life, heavily made up, sexily dressed, provocatively posed.

'Did you want her to be your sister, Johnny?' she asked, unable to hide her distaste.

'You mean she might be a prostitute…like my mother?'

The derisive remark whipped heat into Megan's cheeks—shame at having forgotten what was clearly unforgettable to him. She scrambled to excuse the slip. 'I meant...she doesn't look anything like you.'

'How could I know what *a half-sister* would look like, Megan?'

She took a quick breath, feeling she was drowning in waters too deep for her to wade through. His mother probably hadn't known who *his* father was, let alone...

'I'm sorry, Johnny,' she repeated in frantic appeal. 'I guess...Ric and Mitch are more...more attuned to where you've come from. To me you're just you. And you're such a big person...'

She stopped, shaking her head at the realisation she was denying his past any importance, precisely when he was feeling it very badly. 'What can I do to help?' she cried, horribly conscious of how inadequate that sounded even as the words tripped out of her mouth.

His shoulders squared, his broad chest expanding as he tilted his head back and dragged in a deep breath. 'Let it go.' It was a command to himself. He sighed and his gaze came down to meet hers, eyes bitter with self-mockery. 'Ric has it right. Just let the past go. Stupid of me...in my position...to let myself be sucked in. Sucked back to it.'

He snatched the photograph out of Megan's hand and tore it into smaller and smaller pieces as he stepped over to a wastebin. He dropped the fragments into it and turned to her with a savage look. 'I will never do another concert, Megan. Don't ask it of me again. Not for any reason.'

'I'm sorry...' It sounded so dreadfully ineffec-

tual—as meaningless as a parrot's repetition—but
what else could she say?

'Let's get out of here!'

Security guards escorted them to a limousine.

Security guards rode in the car with them, inhib-
iting any private conversation, not that Johnny's
closed-in demeanor invited any. Megan felt hopelessly inhibited about making any contact at all. She
wished he would hold her hand…anything to link
them again…but he didn't, and the tension emanating from him seemed filled with a fierce impatience
to get this whole business over and done with.

Security guards accompanied them every step of
the way up to Johnny's hotel room, checking it was
empty before they finally withdrew. Even then,
Johnny forestalled any move by Megan to break into
his insulated mood, muttering, 'I need a shower,' and
heading straight for the bathroom. 'Make yourself at
home. Order up some supper if you like. Just call
room service,' he added carelessly.

She was left standing in a very spacious, very lux-
urious hotel suite, overwhelmingly conscious of how
lonely it could be, despite being surrounded by what
great wealth could buy.

Had Johnny felt this kind of loneliness here?
Putting up with it to protect her? Did he feel even
more alone now because she hadn't given him her
complete trust, had stood back from him when she
should have moved forward to offer comfort, assuring him that while he had missed out on much in the
past, she could make up for it?

Megan didn't know if she could or not, but the
strong fear of losing any chance of deep intimacy

with him compelled her into trying to reach out to his heart.

With trembling hands, she stripped off her clothes. Johnny might simply be washing off the sweat from performing under a blast of hot lights, but her imagination saw him washing off the dirty sense of being tricked into facing the murky circumstances of his birth, the horrors of his childhood which he'd never shared with her, drowning out the loneliness that her lack of understanding had undoubtedly made sharper.

She forced her legs to walk into the bathroom, her mind gripping on to a fierce determination not to panic, not to react wimpishly to any suggestion of rejection from Johnny. He didn't hear her enter. He stood under the drenching spray of the shower, eyes closed, head bent, and she saw that the packets of soap provided by the hotel lay unopened, the facecloths still folded on top of the towels.

Grabbing one of the soap packets, she ripped off its wrapping, opened the door to the shower and stepped into the spacious cubicle—plenty of room for two, even with a big man like Johnny. His head snapped up, eyes jerking open.

'You must be exhausted,' Megan rushed out, her own eyes shooting sympathetic appeal as she wildly lathered up her hands. 'Let me…'

She swiftly transferred the suds to his shoulders, spreading them over the tautly bunched muscles, watching them trail down his chest under the beat of the water because she couldn't pluck up the courage to look at his face again, frightened of seeing that he was suffering her touch, not wanting it.

He said nothing but made no move to stop her

from running the soap over him. His stillness and his silence drove her into working quickly, down over his chest, his stomach, lower. The rapid pounding of her own heart drummed in her ears. A desperate desire for him to respond positively slowed her hurrying hands, dictating a more sensual slide over his naked flesh.

I have to make him feel loved, she thought frantically, *not alone, not missing out...*

How could she answer his needs?

Before she could think better of it, a thought slipped out of the anxious jumble in her mind. 'You used to think of me as your little sister.'

She was instantly mortified, realising it sounded like she was linking herself to the blonde who would have done anything to be with him, and here she was caressing him intimately, and he was becoming aroused...

'Megan...' His voice was harsh.

It had been a plea for him to return to caring about her, not...

'You're my wife—' His hands tore hers away from him. *'My wife!'*

'Then let me be your wife,' she cried, her eyes pleading against the angry torment in his. 'I'm sorry I got things wrong. I'm sorry I had no real idea of what the concert involved. I didn't know how it was for you.'

He shook his head in anguish and from his throat came an animal groan of pain. Too bewildered and distressed to fight for anything more, Megan was intensely relieved when he released her hands and pulled her into a fierce embrace, almost crushing the breath out of her. He rubbed his face over her hair. Never mind that it was soaking wet—they were both soaking wet—the action echoed her own craving for him and sent a flood of warmth to her fear-chilled heart.

'You don't need to know,' he growled. 'You'll never need to know. I'm done with it.'

His fingers tangled through her sodden curls and dragged her head back. His eyes blazed into hers. 'But don't you ever think again that I'd choose any other woman over you. Do you hear me, Megan?'

'I'm sorry…'

'No, dammit! Just say yes…yes…'

'Yes.'

His mouth swooped on hers as though he had to taste the word as well as hear it, and Megan poured all her own chaotic emotions into a kiss that pulsated with passionate need—a hot, urgent acceleration of desire that seared away any doubt that Johnny wanted her.

He slammed off the shower faucet, swept her out of the shower cubicle, wrapped a huge bath towel around her, and carried her out to the king-size bed in his hotel suite. There were no pleasure intensifying preliminaries. He came into her hard and fast and Megan welcomed the instant union with as much savage satisfaction as he took in it, a tumultuous fever of possession gripping both of them, whipping them on to a world-shattering climax.

Afterwards she clasped him to her, stroking his hair as he lay with his head resting just above the valley of her breasts, his breath warm against her skin, the tension gone from both of them. He shifted slightly, gliding his hand gently over her rounded belly.

'I forgot the baby,' he murmured incredulously.

'It's all right,' she soothed, smiling over the wonderful fact that he had wanted her so absolutely, not thinking of his child until now. 'I would have told you if it wasn't.'

And right on cue a ripple of movement under her skin reminded them of the new life that would soon be born.

'See…he's kicking me for it,' Johnny said fatuously, a smile in his voice.

'Might be a she.'

'Mmm…' It was a contented hum.

Contentment was good.

Her whole body was humming with it.

Megan didn't want to say anything that might spoil the sense of peaceful harmony, of very real togetherness. She believed Johnny didn't want to be with any other woman, and right now, that was enough.

Whether he really was *done* with his career, or just the concert part of it, she didn't know. Time might change that view anyway. She did know she would respect whatever decision he made about it, no argument, no criticism, no complaint. There might be more needs in Johnny that neither she, nor Gundamurra, nor even their child could ever answer.

He fell asleep, still in her embrace.

She stroked his hair, loving him, determined to be *his wife* in every sense—partner, lover, best friend and confidante. She didn't want him to feel alone…ever again.

CHAPTER FOURTEEN

'HOME...'

So much heartfelt satisfaction in Johnny's voice.

And his grin was pure pleasure.

They were still in the air, flying over the woolshed, the name of the sheep station—Gundamurra—painted in large letters on its roof.

Coming home was all Johnny had talked about ever since they'd woken up in the hotel room this morning. No mention of the concert, nor its traumatic aftermath. It was clear to Megan that he was determined on letting it all go, blocking it out. She wasn't sure if that was right for him, but she wasn't about to cast shadows on the happy twinkle in his eyes.

She grinned back. 'You've still got to get this plane down safely.'

He laughed and brought it in on the airstrip, a perfect landing but for the inevitable bumps along the ground. 'Need to get this strip graded again,' he remarked as he switched off the engine.

Which meant he'd hire a grader in the coming weeks, cost no object to Johnny. Megan didn't worry about what he spent on the property anymore. As long as he was happy.

'Another thing,' he said as they went about disembarking. 'I'm going to buy a helicopter. Emily can teach me how to fly it.'

'Why do you want a helicopter?'

'It would be more handy for checking out the property than a plane. It can land anywhere. And who knows? The Big Wet might come next year and break the drought. It could be raining in January when the baby is due and I want to be able to get you out in time. If the airstrip turns into a bog, we'll need a helicopter.'

She laughed, pleased that he was looking ahead, making plans. 'By all means get yourself a helicopter. And I'm sure Emily will be delighted to give you lessons.'

'Right! Now for Evelyn's superb carrot cake,' he said with relish.

Of course, Evelyn had it ready for him.

And Johnny was in such high good humour he gave her a hug and a kiss on the cheek to thank her for it. 'I love being in your kitchen, Evelyn,' he declared, sitting down at the table, ready to enjoy his afternoon tea. 'This is where I really feel I'm home.'

'Oh, go on with you, Mr Johnny.' She was bridling with pleasure, beaming love right back at him. 'You're just proving the old adage—the way to a man's heart is through his stomach. Here you're served with good home-cooking instead of all that hotel stuff.'

'Only you, Evelyn, can make a cake like this,' he declared, hoeing into the huge slice in front of him.

'Well, that's nice to know. Now tell me how the concert went?'

He shrugged. 'Did its job. Full house. Lots of money for drought relief.'

Evelyn sighed her frustration at what was to her a totally inadequate report. She shot an appealing look at Megan, who knew where Johnny's dismissive attitude was coming from. Nevertheless, it was measly fare for his greatest fan. Impulsively she jumped into the task of giving satisfaction.

'He was wonderful, Evelyn. He had the whole audience—thousands of them—in his hands. The way he used his voice was just magic. They didn't want to let him go when the concert ended, standing up and cheering and clapping. I've never heard anything like it. Absolutely amazing!'

Her warm appreciation of his performance seemed to startle Johnny, jerking his head towards her, but he frowned, too, as though he didn't want to hear it.

'So they should want more,' Evelyn happily declared. 'He's the best singer I've ever heard.'

'Well, they can buy my music anytime they like,' Johnny said carelessly, then switched to a charming smile. '*You* will always have it free, Evelyn. Now please…we're hanging out for news of what's been happening here while we've been away.'

Over and done with, Megan thought.

And Johnny kept it that way.

The weeks rolled on towards Christmas. Megan became more heavily pregnant. Johnny bought his helicopter and learnt to fly it. He took over more of the running of Gundamurra, insisting that she had to slow down and rest, look after herself and the baby.

Quite frequently e-mails came in from his agent who was based in Los Angeles. Johnny read them, answered them, deleted them. He did not discuss them with her, didn't even refer to them. Which Megan found disturbing. The block-out on his career seemed too extreme.

Eventually she felt driven to question him. 'All these e-mails…are you getting offers for work, Johnny?'

'Nothing I want to take up, Megan. I'm finished with all that.' He smiled with grim irony. 'Sooner or later my agent will believe me.'

She let that ride, leaving the decision completely up to him, though she wondered if he would remain content with their life here. Times changed. Currently he was looking forward to being a father, but later down the track…

He shrugged and added, 'Most of the messages are about outstanding business which will roll on for years. Contracts with recording companies and sponsors running out, being re-signed…stuff like that. Nothing for you to worry about.'

'I'm not worried.'

'Good!' He smiled. 'I don't want you to be. I like my life just the way it is, right here with you.'

He meant it and she accepted it, not raising the issue again.

Johnny invited their extended family home for Christmas and they all came. Tradition was upheld with the Christmas Eve party held around the homestead quadrangle, everyone who worked and lived on Gundamurra attending. Johnny took on the role of Santa Claus, giving out gifts he'd bought personally and piled under the Christmas tree with almost childish delight, anticipating the surprise and pleasure they'd give when unwrapped.

It made Megan wonder how many miserable Christmases he'd spent as a boy. Empty times. Lonely times. And she thought how much her father's understanding had encompassed when he'd opened his heart and mind and home to his three bad boys, turning their lives around, teaching them there were different paths to take—paths far more rewarding to their true inner selves.

'If anyone can fill Mr Patrick's shoes, it's Mr Johnny,' Evelyn whispered to Megan, almost bursting with pride in her personal favourite, watching him charm the children with 'Ho-ho-hos' as he made much of selecting just the right gift for them.

But would filling those huge shoes answer what Johnny truly wanted for himself?

Megan remembered what Mitch had said when she'd been so angry over the terms of her father's will, carrying on about Johnny being a pop-star—

You've just pasted a label on the man which I know to be very superficial, Megan. Johnny has not yet reached the fulfilment of the person he is.

And yes, it had been a superficial label, meanly judged. Her father, Mitch and Ric had known Johnny far more deeply. She was still learning about the person he was, knew that fatherhood would be something big in his life, but where true fulfilment lay for him, she didn't know. Perhaps he didn't know himself yet. She could only hope it lay in their life at Gundamurra.

Regretful of her lack of generosity towards him in the past and far more aware of his childhood background, she'd bought him many gifts for Christmas; a new Akubra hat, a leather belt with the letter *G* for Gundamurra worked into the buckle, a coffee mug with Daddy printed on it, a big enough possum harness for him to wear if he wanted to carry the baby with him as he walked around the station, a box of chocolates to feed his sweet tooth. She had another, more important gift for him, waiting for when they could be alone together.

Johnny gave her a beautiful pearl ring which he'd bought secretly while they were on their honeymoon in Broome. Megan loved it. Somehow it made the gift of the pearl necklace for her twenty-first birthday far more personal and special.

After the usual massive feast on Christmas day, when everyone else was tottering off to have a siesta through the heat of the afternoon, she drew Johnny along the verandah to the office. Although she felt nervous that he might feel pressured to be what she wanted him to be, the gift still felt right to her.

She handed him the prepared envelope.

In it lay the deed to two percent of Gundamurra from her share, giving him the controlling hand.

He stared at it, frowned, and panic instantly played havoc with Megan's taut nerves. He turned an uncomprehending look to her. 'Why?'

'Without you, Gundamurra would not have survived. And you're my husband, Johnny. It's...it's more fitting that you be the boss.'

He shook his head. 'Patrick's will...'

'My father chose you to play the role of knight to the rescue and you did it very generously. But it's moved beyond that now, Johnny. We're married. I think Dad would give his blessing to this gift.' Her argument faltered into uncertainty. 'Do you... Do you mind?'

He threw out his hands. 'How could I mind?' Yet he still frowned, searching her eyes. 'Are you sure you want to give this, Megan? I know how much inheriting Gundamurra meant to you.'

A painful flush scorched her cheeks. She'd been so hateful to him over the will, scornful of all he'd stood for in her eyes, fiercely rejecting any encroachment by him on what she saw as her territory.

'I was wrong, Johnny. Wrong about so many things…' Her apologetic smile was tinged with irony. 'You've shown me how wrong I was and I want to make up for it.' Her eyes begged him to let her.

'Megan…' He sighed, then moved to curl his hands around her shoulders, his eyes warmly reassuring. 'You're Patrick's daughter. You didn't need to do this. I don't feel less of a man because you own more of Gundamurra than I do. This gift is too big for me to accept. I can't feel right about it.'

'But I feel right to give it,' she pleaded. Or was she subconsciously tying him to her? Loading him with a responsibility to stop him from ever walking away? Trying to balance out her own secret insecurities?

He hesitated, assessing her need, weighing it against what he felt. Finally he said. 'Then let it be one percent. Equal partners.' He grinned. 'I can live very happily with that.'

Relief poured through her. 'Partners. Yes,' she eagerly agreed, winding her arms around his neck, pulling his head down to draw him into a kiss which would seal their partnership—a kiss that very quickly led to Johnny sweeping her off to bed.

They gave Mitch the job of fixing the percentage for them.

Their baby was born three weeks after Christmas—an adorable little girl whom they named Jennifer, instantly shortened to Jenny by her doting father.

The drought had not broken. Johnny's helicopter wasn't needed to transport Megan to and from the maternity ward in Bourke hospital. However, they were no sooner back on Gundamurra when the rain did come, and it was a Big Wet, raining on and off for the next two months. The parched country, that had seemed so lifeless for so long, started to bloom again.

'It's like a miracle, isn't it?' Johnny remarked with awe as they stood on the front verandah one morning, looking out on grassed land that reached to the horizon.

'Rebirth,' she murmured, loving how it always happened—what looked like dead ground coming to life again.

'Two miracles,' Johnny crooned down at their daughter who was cradled in his arms. 'You came into the world and brought the rain with you, Jenny. Now we'll be able to build up a whole army of sheep. Lots of lambs for you to play with.'

She gurgled back at him, perfectly happy with her father's plan. And Megan, too, was perfectly happy. No doubts at all that Johnny was happy to make his life on Gundamurra with her and their child.

No doubts…until she watched Johnny's movie on the night before Good Friday.

The weather had turned fine enough for the family to fly in for Easter, an invitation pressed by Johnny so he could show off his daughter. Ric brought *the surprise* with him—a video copy of *The Last Cowboy Standing,* which had already been released in the U.S. and according to Ric, was grossing huge box office profits.

'You're slaying them, Johnny,' he said with huge pride in his old friend. 'I've just been in L.A. on business, and believe me, even the diehard critics are hailing you as an actor who should be up for an Academy Award for this performance.'

'That's just hype,' Johnny demurred.

'Well, let's see,' Mitch drawled, grinning from ear to ear as he added, 'Can't wait to watch John Wayne riding again.'

Everyone stood up, eager to go to the TV room. They'd finished dinner. The children were in bed asleep. There was no reasonable excuse not to watch the movie and it would be like another rejection of Johnny if she didn't, yet Megan could not quell the fear that Ric's report had stirred. If Johnny's acting was so good…she didn't want to see, didn't want to know.

He'd put aside his singing career. She could accept that because he had already achieved his ambitions in that arena, but this might be another career pinnacle he'd want to climb. They'd been so happy together these past few months. She didn't want anything to threaten what they now shared, but wasn't that being mean again, thinking only of what *she* wanted instead of considering Johnny's needs?

If she had to, she'd go with him anywhere.

He caught her hand as they were heading out of the dining room, pausing her while the others moved on, squeezing it hard as he murmured, 'Are you okay with this, Megan?'

She looked up into eyes that were sharp with concern, caring about what she felt, caring which was undoubtedly fed by the bad memories she'd given him.

'Of course,' she replied, smiling to show they would not be in conflict over this movie or anything arising out of it.

Still he hesitated, apparently reluctant to see himself in the movie, anyway.

'Have you got a problem with it?' she asked, wondering if he'd been intent on blocking out everything he'd done before their marriage.

He grimaced. 'I've never watched myself perform.'

Embarrassment that he might not live up to the hype?

'You're brilliant onstage, Johnny,' she assured him, squeezing *his* hand to inject her support and confidence. 'You have a talent for emoting that I'm sure will come across on film, too.'

'Emoting...' He looked quizzically at her for a moment, then shrugged. 'Well, might as well see what the director did with all the scenes he shot. Just remember it's only a movie, Megan. Okay?'

'Okay,' she repeated firmly.

There had to be a woman in it, Megan thought, as they followed the others to the TV room. The tension emanating from Johnny probably meant there were love scenes. But she was not going to be jealous. The movie had been made before they were married. Johnny's commitment to her since then had been rock-solid. She fervently wished she hadn't doubted it over the blonde at the concert. So many wrongs...still to be righted.

One of the sofas had been left vacant for them. As soon as they were settled on it, Ric started the video rolling. The credits zigzagged over a long shot of a cowboy riding towards a ranch. Ric and Mitch tossed a few teasing remarks at Johnny which he took good-humouredly. However, everyone was stunned into silence when the cowboy finally reached home and entered the ranch house.

Silence from the movie, too. No music track. No speech. Just the stark images of a wife who had been beaten, raped, and killed, and two small children lying broken and dead on the floor, blood on the wall showing where their head injuries had happened. The shock and grief of the cowboy were heart-gripping and everyone watching could see—feel—the surge of savage need to find the perpetrators, grim purpose mixed with a terrible tenderness as he removed a red and white polka dot neckerchief from his wife's dead grasp.

He crushed it in his own hand and that image was instantly transferred to the cowboy standing at three graves, slowly turning away and walking to his horse. Then the music started—music that seemed to reinforce the relentless beat of the horse's hooves, riding out on an unshakeable mission.

'Hell!' Ric breathed. 'That's powerful stuff, Johnny.'

To Megan every scene that followed was power-ful; each gang member being hunted, confronted, punished with raging violence, then killed, until there was only one left, the leader who'd worn the neckerchief. No longer having the support of the others, he panicked and rode away. During the chase, the cowboy was shot and badly wounded, though he managed to keep riding and reach another ranch house where he collapsed at the front door.

When he swam back to consciousness, two small children came into view, clearly stirring anguished memories, then the woman who'd taken him in and was tending his wound, a widow who was struggling to survive on the ranch.

She let him know he was an unwelcome intrusion, an extra burden she resented, but he gradually thawed her hostile attitude with how kindly and caringly he treated her children who lapped up his attention. Sexual tension grew as the cowboy recovered and on the night before he was to leave, the widow decided to have him, well aware that the probability was he'd never come back.

It was an extraordinary scene—the cowboy's sense that it wasn't right to take what she was offering, the torment on his face, the widow goading him into succumbing to the desire they both felt, a kind of desperate passion in the lovemaking. It gave Megan goose bumps, reminding her of her own feelings on the night Jenny had been conceived.

The next morning the children followed the cowboy to his horse, pleading for him to come back soon, but the widow simply stood in the doorway, watching him go with a bleak look of resignation on her face.

He hunted down the gang leader, but there was no explosion of violence, no fury, more a grim execution. The cowboy dropped the polka dot square of cloth over his dead face with an air of sick finality. His expression clearly telegraphed—done, but what to do with his life now? He rode back to the graves of his family. More poignant grief and a sense of saying goodbye as the crosses of the graves were silhouetted by a beautiful sunset.

The final shot was of the widow's children, spotting a cowboy riding towards their ranch, calling out to their mother, running to meet him and the widow coming to the doorway, a frown gradually lifting to an expression of wonderment as the cowboy dismounted, took the children's hands, and walked towards her.

Megan was still mopping up tears when Ric turned the television off. Her sisters and Lara and Kathryn were, too. Even Mitch had to clear his throat before speaking.

'No hype, Johnny. You made me live that with you.'

'Yeah,' Ric agreed, shaking his head in bemusement. 'There's nothing new about the story-line— probably been done a thousand times—yet you made it so personal. It's your movie, Johnny. You carried it all the way and made it a great movie. A *tour de force*. No wonder you're getting rave reviews!'

'Probably surprise more than anything,' Johnny mocked.

'How do *you* feel about it?' Lara inserted quietly.

He grimaced. 'Makes me feel I've been caught naked, to tell you the truth. I shouldn't have done it.' He pushed up from the sofa, drawing Megan to her feet, as well. 'If you don't mind, you guys, I'm taking my wife off to bed. Jenny still wakes up at night.'

My wife…and Jenny, his child…

Megan was acutely conscious of the silence they left behind them, even more conscious of Johnny's rejection of his acting which had been so good it could very well lead him to be a megastar on the screen.

He was closing himself off from it because of her and their child. Megan had passively accepted his decision to retire from the entertainment field, but now she felt very strongly that it wasn't right for him to turn his back on so much talent. It was too big a sacrifice…a terrible waste.

She had to talk to him about it.

Had to open the doors.

She remembered him quoting Shakespeare the morning after her father's wake—

'And one man in his time plays many parts.'

If anyone should, that person was Johnny Ellis.

CHAPTER FIFTEEN

MEGAN sat on their bed, watching her husband strip off his clothes, remembering the scene he'd played with the widow in the movie—the raw conflict and the caring.

'Why are you embarrassed?' she asked.

He shot her a wary look, eyes guarded, watchful, assessing.

Anticipating trouble with her?

'Mitch was right,' she asserted warmly. 'You made us live it with you. I don't think many actors can grab people by the throat like that. You deserve the accolades, Johnny.'

A wry little smile twitched at his mouth. 'I wasn't really acting, Megan. I just channelled what I felt about...other things...into the role.'

'What other things?' she probed, her pulse skipping into a faster beat at the implication that parts of the movie had parallelled his own life experience.

Caught naked...

He shook his head. 'None of it relates to our life now.'

Putting in the block again.

Megan gritted her teeth, determined to fight it this time. 'I want to know all of you, Johnny, not just the part you think is suitable for me.'

He flashed her a hard look. 'No, you don't, Megan. You've spelled out many times that Gundamurra is your world and you don't want to be a part of any other.'

Damned by her own words!

'I'm sorry that the movie has disturbed you,' he went on. 'Just remember it was made *before* we were married.'

Her own thoughts before she saw it!

Her heart sank as she realised Johnny had taken on board all the parameters she had drawn and because he wanted their marriage to work, he was doing what he had to do to keep it within them. In a burst of shattering insight, she understood it was the mind-set of a survivor. Cut away anything that might put their life together at risk. Keep everything steady and on course. Don't invite trouble. Be charming. Smile.

The abused child in Johnny Ellis was still there—buried deep but still inside him, doing what had to be done to survive and prosper in a hostile world!

Having shed his clothes, he landed on the bed, pulled her down beside him, and *smiled* to set her at ease as he started unbuttoning her shirt. 'You must be tired...'

'Stop!' she cried.

He frowned at the sharpness of her protest.

'Stop patronising me, Johnny.' Her eyes begged his understanding as she rushed to explain. 'I did see your career as a threat to anything we could have together, but I have grown up this past year and I know to put someone like you in a cage is terribly wrong.'

The frown returned. 'I'm not caged at Gundamurra, Megan. There's plenty of space here.

Different challenges. More than enough to happily occupy me.'

She reached up and stroked his cheek, wanting desperately to get under his skin, the self-protective layers he'd grown over too many years. 'I love you, Johnny. I want you to share your life with me. All of it, not just the part you think is acceptable to me. I promise you, I won't turn away from any of it, just because it's unfamiliar to me. So please…put down the barriers and let me into your mind.'

His eyes studied hers quizzically. 'You've never said that before.'

'I've been a frightened fool, holding back because I didn't believe I could ever have all of you, but if you'll truly share with me, Johnny, I swear I'll always be there for you, wherever you want to go and whatever you want to do. I'll never take your family from you, nor…'

He placed gentle fingers on her lips, halting her speech. 'You love me?' he repeated gruffly, as though that was all he'd heard.

Appalled that he had gone all this time with her in the intimacy of their marriage and not felt loved, Megan spilled out the truth of her long fixation on him, from when she was a little girl—her hero-worship, her teenage crush, the self-protective rejection that had taken the form of scorn, the wild intensity of her need to have him *once,* the guilt of *trapping* him into marriage, the fear of not ever being enough for him. She laid her heart absolutely bare, desperately hoping he would open up, too—good or bad.

She had to know.

Only with knowing could she feel truly married to him.

No secrets.

No forbidden areas.

Honesty.

She saw her revelations strike chords of recognition in his eyes, saw them provoke expressions of bemusement, tenderness, regret, irony, and her nerves were screwed into a complete mess by the time she'd laid it all out to him, but she didn't care. It was the truth.

For several heart-churning moments he made no reply, simply stroking the wild mop of her hair away from her face, seemingly entranced by the curly tendrils. Or the colour. Her crowning glory.

'We always had that gap between us, Megan,' he remarked ruefully. 'You captured my heart when you were a little girl. In my mind, I adopted you as my little sister, just as I adopted Patrick as my father. Crossing that line was unthinkable. Though I certainly thought about it in recent years.'

'You did?' she queried incredulously.

He nodded.

'You never showed it.'

'Inappropriate. Firstly, you were Patrick's daughter. Secondly, you wouldn't have a bar of me, anyway.'

She sighed. 'I thought you were out of my reach, Johnny.'

'I realise that now. But once you agreed to our making love on the night of Patrick's wake, I was hell-bent on bridging that gap.'

That startled her into saying, 'It wasn't…just sex?'

A whimsical little smile. 'Did it feel like *just sex* to you?'

'Johnny, I was so caught up in my own feelings…and I'd baited you, tricked you…'

'I was where I wanted to be, Megan. And nothing was going to stop me from coming back and winning more from you.'

'Like…in the movie?' she asked, wanting to know if he'd transferred his feelings for her to the scene with the widow.

He grimaced. 'I didn't think of you ever seeing that movie. When I went back to Arizona, I had them rewrite the part with the widow. I could see she should be thinking the cowboy had too big a commitment to his previous life, that he'd go and never come back. You were in my head all the time, Megan.'

'The cowboy was torn by the situation, too, Johnny—between her and what he'd set out to do,' she reminded him. 'I don't want you to feel torn.'

'It was something he had to finish before he could move on. And he did finish it. I feel the same way. There's no conflict in me about what I want.' He smiled, a beautiful, happy smile. 'You've just given it to me.'

Her love…

Such a powerful thing if it wasn't hemmed in by constrictions.

'It's free, Johnny,' she promised him. 'You don't have to perform for me. No matter what you choose to do, or have done in the past, I love you.'

'What still bothers you about my past, Megan?'

'The children…what you felt in the movie. You said you channelled it…from what?'

Sadness clouded his eyes. 'When you're a little kid, you can't stop what adults do,' he said quietly. 'I remember Ric telling Mitch and me—back when we were sixteen—how his mother was regularly beaten up and eventually killed by his father, how he'd tried to get in the way, only to get hurled aside and beaten himself. I knew how that was. I learnt very young that you can't win against adults. They're too strong. And they have answers for everything— for the bruises and the broken bones and the bedwetting…'

'What was the worst for you?'

He hesitated, not wanting to pull it out.

'You told me about Ric, Johnny,' she quickly pressed. 'Please…tell me about you.'

It came reluctantly, almost as though he was ashamed of it. 'Being hit wasn't so bad. I hated being locked in a cupboard. Alone. In the dark. No escape. Days, nights…I never knew how long it would last. Or if they'd forget I was there. I had to stay quiet or I'd get pulled out, beaten, and put back even longer.'

'My God, Johnny! No wonder you ran away when you could.'

'It's a long way behind me now,' he said dismissively. 'But playing that initial scene in the movie— the terrible waste of lives that promised so much— it wasn't hard for me to call up grief, nor a savage desire to balance the ledger. Though, in the end, as Ric says, it's best to let those feelings go and move on. You just don't ever forget…how it was.'

'No,' she murmured. 'I can't imagine you would.

Thank you for telling me. It helps me to bridge the gap...knowing why you think and feel as you do. And I don't want you to ever feel alone again, Johnny.'

He smiled as she wound her arms around his neck, the desire for more unifying action simmering into his eyes as he hopefully asked, 'Have I said enough?'

'No.'

'What more?' His patience was being tested.

'I want to hear you say you love me.'

He laughed, and to Megan's ears, it was the heady laugh of freedom. His eyes sparkled wild pleasure as he bent to brush his lips over hers and whisper, 'I love you, Megan Maguire. I love having you as my partner in all things. I love sharing your life—'

'You've got to let me share yours, too,' she cut in breathlessly.

'Everything. I love everything about you.'

Then he proceeded to show her how very much he did, and she loved him right back...openly, wholeheartedly, blissfully secure in the certain knowledge that she was every bit as special to him as he was to her...and always would be.

CHAPTER SIXTEEN

JOHNNY was completely at peace with his world the next morning, looking benevolently on everyone, not the least bit perturbed when Mitch and Ric wanted a private meeting with him in the office. As the three of them strolled along the verandah which skirted the inner quadrangle of the homestead, he inquired about his old friends' contentment with their lives.

'I'm a happy man,' Ric declared.

'Couldn't have it better,' Mitch said decisively.

'Sorry if I did wrong, bringing that video, Johnny,' Ric slung at him with an edge of concern. 'Didn't mean to upset things.'

'You didn't,' Johnny assured him. 'It cut a bit close to the bone in places, but that's all right.'

'You're okay with it?'

'Sure.'

'Megan?'

'No problem. Sorted a few things out for us, actually. Guess I was a bit too tight-lipped about stuff I've carried with me for a long time.'

'I was with Kathryn, too,' Mitch admitted ruefully. 'Hard to open up. But makes a big difference when you do.'

'Makes sense of everything for them,' Ric remarked knowingly.

So they had held back, too, Johnny thought.

We all felt vulnerable…guarding ourselves.

Trust was such a huge thing, coming from their backgrounds. They'd learnt to trust Patrick. Yet even he, at the end, had confounded Johnny with his will. Probably Mitch and Ric, too, though they'd set it aside, making up their own reasons for it.

'So what's this meeting about?' he asked as he ushered them into the office.

'A letter from Patrick,' Mitch answered.

Johnny was stunned. He closed the door on automatic pilot, staring at the other two. It was clear they both knew about it. No surprise on Ric's face. And Mitch was drawing an envelope out from inside the jacket he was wearing.

'He left it with me, Johnny,' he explained. 'To be opened a year after his death when the three of us were together.'

Fair enough, Johnny thought. Mitch was the lawyer. Of course he would obey Patrick's instructions. Yet if it explained the will, why a year later? It would have saved a huge amount of heartburn and worry if they'd all known Patrick's reasoning in the first place.

Mitch held out the envelope. 'I think you should read it out, Johnny.'

'No. He put it in your keeping, Mitch,' he asserted, his stomach already churning over what its contents might be, whether Patrick would have wanted what he'd ultimately done. The other two had nothing to worry about. They could be at ease, while he… No, he fiercely told himself. He'd done right. It felt right. Megan felt it, too. Partners, in every sense.

'You read it, Mitch,' Ric agreed.

None of them moved to sit down. Somehow, it

was a mark of respect to Patrick to keep standing.
Mitch opened the envelope and withdrew a sheet of
paper, slowly unfolding it. He cleared his throat.

'Just let me read it through. Leave any discussion
of its contents to the end. Agreed?'

Johnny and Ric nodded.

Mitch took a deep breath and read—

My three sons,

*That's how I think of you. I could not have loved
you more, nor been more proud of you, if you had
been born to me.*

*I get so tired now. I can feel my body slowing
down, time running out. Ric and Mitch, both of you
have found what you needed to fulfil the rich promise
of your lives. I believe you know this and will understand I want the same for Johnny. To some measure, I think I stood in the way of that happening, so
the will I have written is meant to correct that.*

*There's Megan, too. I've made provision for Jessie
and Emily but Megan will need help to get past this
drought and rebuild. I know all three of you would
step forward to ensure her future on Gundamurra,
but I have singled out Johnny, not because I favour
him above either of you, but because it gives him my
approval and blessing to make his home at
Gundamurra with Megan, if he so wishes.*

*I sit here thinking of the bond that has always been
between them—a natural gravitation towards each
other which has never lessened, though it has been
much strained in recent years. I believe the tension
I have observed between them is the tension of barriers raised which neither of them feel able to cross.*

I could be wrong. A year is long enough to break

*those barriers if the desire to do so has the strength
of love behind it. If this has not proved true, I now
put it in the hands of the three of you to correct the
inheritance, returning it all to Megan, and sharing
the financial onus I put on Johnny to rescue
Gundamurra for her.*

*You each offered help. I know it's in your hearts
to give it. Let Johnny go free to seek what I hope he
will find one day—the peace of coming home to a
woman he loves, who also loves him. And Johnny,
please forgive my trespass on your life. I trust the
year was not too hard on you. On all three of you,
wondering why I did what I've done.*

*Stay brothers to each other. And thank you for all
you have given me through the years.*

Patrick.

It took Johnny a while to swallow the lump in his
throat, to feel composed enough to speak. 'Did either
of you realise what the will was about?'

'We didn't know for sure, Johnny,' Ric answered.
'We just figured Patrick knew what he was doing.'

'Knight attack,' Mitch murmured, waving to the
chess table. 'Patrick wanted you to capture the queen.
That seemed to be the logic of it. And you did,
Johnny.'

'Well, I wouldn't put it like that to Megan,' he
said hotly. 'We're partners.'

'All the barriers down?' Ric quizzed, a satisfied
twinkle lurking in his brilliant dark eyes. 'Seemed
that way to me this morning.'

A quick train of realizations clicked through
Johnny's head. 'That damned concert! Lara's idea.

And bringing a video of the movie home, shoving it in our faces...'

'You helped me with Lara, Johnny,' came the quick retort.

'You *knew* something, Ric.'

'I swear I just put two and two together.'

'We were both here for Megan's twenty-first birthday,' Mitch slid in. 'It was very clear that we didn't make up for your absence.'

'Right! So I'm an idiot for not seeing it before this.'

'No, Johnny. Megan was ten years younger than you. And Patrick's daughter,' came the sympathetic reply. 'They were big blinkers to see past. Both Ric and I wore the same blinkers until Patrick's will was read. Then for the most part we stood back and let the two of you fight it out.'

'Which brings us to the critical question...' Ric paused, then pointedly inquired, 'Have you come home, Johnny?'

'Yes. Yes, I have.'

And he laughed because they were both grinning at him, and their grins plainly said, 'Welcome to the club!'

'In fact,' he went on, 'I was discussing with Megan last night—I'd like to start up an opportunity program for street-kids here on Gundamurra. I probably won't be as good as Patrick at it, but I want to give it a shot.'

'No question kids would relate to you, Johnny,' Mitch said warmly. 'It's a great idea.'

'Very fitting,' Ric agreed. He nodded to the big leather chair behind the desk. 'If anyone can fill

Patrick's chair, it's you, Johnny. I wish you well with it.'

'I'll second that,' Mitch said, smiling. 'I can see that chair fitting you like a glove as time goes on.'

It embarrassed Johnny that they thought so much of him, but he was intensely grateful for their support and understanding. 'Thanks, guys. I'll do my best to live up to it. And Mitch, I was thinking since you're high up in legal circles, you could help me organise the program.'

'You can certainly count on my help.'

'I take it you're not thinking of doing any more movies?' Ric posed.

'No. It's not real life. What I have with Megan here on Gundamurra *is* real. And it's good. I wouldn't swap it for anything.'

'So there's nothing to discuss,' Mitch said decisively. 'I think we should do what all brothers would do at such a time. Arm ourselves with a drink and raise a toast to the man who got it right for us.'

Which they proceeded to do.

'To Patrick Maguire, who gave us the lives we now have,' Ric said.

'To the best father we could have had,' Mitch said.

'Rest in peace, Patrick. It was indeed a *good day* when we arrived at Gundamurra,' Johnny said. Then with deep feeling, 'Your mission is complete. We've all come home.'

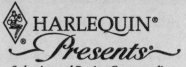

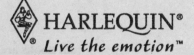

If you enjoyed what you just read,
then we've got an offer you can't resist!

Take 2 bestselling
love stories FREE!
Plus get a FREE surprise gift!

Clip this page and mail it to Harlequin Reader Service®

IN U.S.A.	IN CANADA
3010 Walden Ave.	P.O. Box 609
P.O. Box 1867	Fort Erie, Ontario
Buffalo, N.Y. 14240-1867	L2A 5X3

YES! Please send me 2 free Harlequin Presents® novels and my free surprise
gift. After receiving them, if I don't wish to receive anymore, I can return the
shipping statement marked cancel. If I don't cancel, I will receive 6 brand-new
novels every month, before they're available in stores! In the U.S.A., bill me at
the bargain price of $3.80 plus 25¢ shipping & handling per book and
applicable sales tax, if any*. In Canada, bill me at the bargain price of $4.47 plus
25¢ shipping & handling per book and applicable taxes**. That's the complete
price and a savings of at least 10% off the cover prices—what a great deal! I
understand that accepting the 2 free books and gift places me under no
obligation ever to buy any books. I can always return a shipment and cancel at
any time. Even if I never buy another book from Harlequin, the 2 free books and
gift are mine to keep forever.

106 HDN DZ7Y
306 HDN DZ7Z

Name	(PLEASE PRINT)	
Address	Apt.#	
City	State/Prov.	Zip/Postal Code

Not valid to current Harlequin Presents® subscribers.

Want to try two free books from another series?
Call 1-800-873-8635 or visit www.morefreebooks.com.

* Terms and prices subject to change without notice. Sales tax applicable in N.Y.
** Canadian residents will be charged applicable provincial taxes and GST.
   All orders subject to approval. Offer limited to one per household.
   ® are registered trademarks owned and used by the trademark owner and or its licensee.

PRES04R   ©2004 Harlequin Enterprises Limited

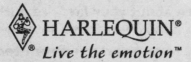

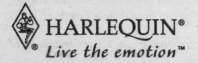